ALSO BY JALEN TELLIS

NightFall: Stories

Reckoning: A Novella

SAMURAI REBORN

The Black Samurai

THE BLACK SAMURAI TRILOGY
BOOK I

JALEN TELLIS

SAMURAI REBORN: THE BLACK SAMURAI
Previously published as a Jalen Tellis hardcover and paperback in January 2024
Second Edition Jalen Tellis paperback printing

Contact: visionaryproductionbusiness@gmail.com

Editor: Lori R

Paperback ISBN:

INTRODUCTION

Genji Sato is an African-American samurai raised in the Japanese culture. He has a tragic past, which leaves him feeling hopeless and lost as a child. But now, as an adult, he tries to forget most of it. Growing up in Koawa, his father, Ken Sato, the protector and leader of The Majo Clan, helped guide him to become a samurai when the time was right.

Years later, a tragedy happens between them and the enemies " The Rudo Clan" and Takashi Kuri, the ruler. The tragedy led to the death of Ken Sato, making Genji go through a journey of vengeance.

Genji is now a vicious, blood-lusted, rageful human being who seeks revenge for his people and his father's death. He wants to honor his father's legacy; he feels that going through this vengeful mission will help achieve that.

I am dedicated to my family for supporting me throughout everything.

"Revenge is self-defeating. It will eat away you until there is nothing left."

— Chris Bradford

PROLOGUE: KOAWA, SUMMER 2017

It is the one time of year when everyone is out enjoying themselves and feels hopeful and joyful. Every summer, The Bushido Matsuri always comes into play. It is a beautiful festival where all Civilians walk around, enjoying everyone's company, and have the chance to worship and honor spirits and gods—vendors on the sidewalks across the villages, the remarkable air of fresh foods in the atmosphere. An innocent sound of laughs comes from the little ones running around as their next of kens chase after them. As for the protectors of Koawa, the Majo Clan took this chance at the festival to honor their deceased brothers, remembering their honor and will. It's the only time of year when they're not working, focusing on protecting the village. They stand, relax, chat, laugh, smile—not worrying about anything.

The silky, smooth collusion of sky bursts red and yellows into the calm of night in the back as the light in Koawa flashes, brightening up the village and turning the visuals into perfection. Music is playing in the background, sounding beautiful, harmonious, rhythmic, and soothing. People gather in a circle, watching dancers performing Kenbu 剣舞. The spark of interest in everyone. Their eyes were caught by the woman's light Yukata's, moving smoothly with the katana on their side and their Sensu as they moved it around in the motion.

While the people in Koawa are out, having the time of their lives. Among the buildings from afar from the festivals, almost a few blocks away. A nearby dojo, The Majo Dojo, is what they call it—the place where all of the Samurai members of The Majo Clan go and train. Sensei teaches younger generations the way of the samurai. Silence is all you can hear inside the dojo, away from the loud noises. A young man, Genji Sato, seventeen years old, six feet tall, wearing his Kimono set gown, as he trains in the middle of the mat. The mat was modern white, with the interior walls darkened as the Majo Clan logo was in the center. He was focused, his eyes closed, and he couldn't hear anything but his thoughts. He was training with his katana as he swung it back and forth, grunting after every vicious swing he threw.

"I see you have gotten better with your stance," says someone as they stood in front of the doorway, observing Genji as he was training. After hearing the familiar voice, Genji stops in his tracks. He opened his eyes to look to his right to see where the voice was coming from.

" Father," Genji says, " Sorry, I didn't think anyone would be in the dojo."

" Well, I was looking for you. I thought you'd be participating in the festival like everyone else." The father said.

" You know, the festivals aren't my type of thing, Father," Genji replied.

" That's understandable, but I see your priorities are elsewhere," The father says as he looks around the dojo. " I see a great improvement from last week. You've been training outside of lessons, haven't you?"

" I have," Genji replies; he looks down at the mat as his voice trembles, fearing getting into trouble. Training outside of lessons was prohibited. The senseis want everyone who is training to be at an equal level. " I'm sorry, father. I know I shouldn't be training outside lessons, especially during the Bushido Matsuri."

" Is it because of what happened yesterday?" The father asked.

" Will it be embarrassing if I said yes?" Genji replies to the question with a question. The father chuckles, finding it amusing, but cuts off the laughter.

" There's nothing to be embarrassed about of losing a sparing match, Genji. Sakura had the upper hand."

That moment still hurts Genji, making him feel like a failure for losing. " It was more than just a sparing match," Genji says, putting his katana towards his side and giving his father full attention as he stands up straight. " Sakura has been the only student in the class that I can't beat. And every time she beats me, she always rubs it in my face."

" You two and this rivalry. I won't be surprised if you two fight to the death one day," the father said. " Don't let that determine your skills, son. There's no need to overtrain."

" How else am I going to get better?" Genji asked. "The only person who can improve me is myself."

"That's correct," The father says. " But remember, if you're hard on yourself, you stop yourself from getting better."

The advice changed the room, leaving Genji with something to think about. The room was silent momentarily, both men not saying anything as the slight sounds were coming from afar at the festival. The father was giving his son slack and not being too hard on him. He sees great intentions from him, but his mindset is still going through a process.

" I understand, father," Genji Says. " Thank you."

" Of course, my son, now save the training for the lessons, understand?"

" Yes, father."

" Good, now come. I need you to help me with something," the father said as he walked away from the dojo. Genji obeyed his father as he walked out of the dojo without hesitation.

Genji runs and catches up with him, now beginning to walk side by side, heading towards the center of the village where the festival is being held.

"What do you need, father?" asks Genji.

"I just need a little help getting water so that I can help the people at the farm plant their vegetables," the father replied.

"They're still having trouble planting?"

"Not anymore. When they just ran out of resources, they couldn't, but thankfully, Tano and I were able to bring some new ones from the other Clans villages."

"That's good," Genji says. " It must've been easy."

"Certain clans seem very strict by letting outsiders into their villages."

" But you are a leader and a protector. Why don't they trust you?" Genji asked curiously.

" Sometimes, Genji, clans are not allies. As you age, you will understand that not everybody in different groups is looking for alliances," the father replies. "Some are just looking for peace and stability. Some are looking for chaos and conflict. Some are just looking for greed and power."

Genji looked at his father. His curiosity was pure. He wanted to know more about the samurai's intentions and what they sought. His father talked about every other group, but what was he looking for? " What about you?" Genji asked him. "What are you and The Majo Clan looking for?"

It took his father a moment to respond. His silence made Genji feel tense as if he had said something wrong. His father came to a stop and put his hand on Genji's chest to make him stop in his tracks as well. He turned and looked at Genji; the face of a severe man struck fear into Genji.

" For generations, even before I became leader of The Majo Clan. We have only been looking for one thing, and that is the purpose," His father said. " As the protectors, we have the purpose of helping the ones who can't help themselves and fighting for the ones who can't fight back themselves. And also, we train the youth to become the next generation of leaders and warriors. But my personal purpose is to make sure I guide you on the right path. The path of greatness."

His speech sparked Genji's interest, and he smiled at his father. Genji looks up to him very much, the way he listens, responds, and acts. Their blood may not be the same, but their love for each other is no different. Genji puts his hand on his father's shoulder, making intense eye contact. " Wanna know my purpose?" Genji asked. " Is to be like you. Be the leader of The Majo Clan one day, and walk in your footsteps. I've been doing it for so long; I want to make you proud."

His father puts his hand on Genji's shoulder, looking at him intensely. " I already am proud of you, my son." His father says. "But, don't live your whole life trying to be someone else. You have to build your legacy. Understand."

" I understand..." Genji says confidently.

" Okay, now let's get moving, I don't want the people at the farm waiting."

—

As they both walk into the festival, everyone screams excitedly as they see them both. They were greeted, hugged, and waved at as they passed. The moon was visible, shining through as the festival lights were purely magical. A bright flashing lights started beaming from the sky. Genji and his father looked up, and everyone jumped in excitement. The Hanabi taikai begin to start.

Genji and Ken finally arrive at the farm. Three of the farmers are on the land: one is raking the grass, and the other two are putting bits of their plants in their big grey wheelbarrow. As Genji and his father walk on the farm, they all notice their visitors and stop what they are doing to greet them. " Mr. Sato, it's a pleasure to see you here," says one of the farmers. "And you too, Genji."

" It's a pleasure to be here helping you all out. You still need assistance on grabbing water?" Genji's father asked.

" Yes, that would mean a lot, Mr. Sato."

" Of course, and please call me Ken! You have known me since I was little. We're practically family." Ken says.

" As my protector, Mr. Sato, you deserve the utmost respect." The farmer says, which makes Ken smile slightly.

The farmer hands Ken a large bucket to put the water in. Ken hands it to Genji, insisting he start and prepare to do the job himself. " Here you go, Genji. You know where the lake is, right?" Ken asks.

" Yes," Genji replied.

" Good, just get some water and come back here to the farm."

Right before Genji was about to walk off, Ken and he heard a familiar voice shout from afar. " There you too are," someone said. Ken and Genji turned behind, seeing their good alliance; Tano, one of the members of The Majo Clan, walked toward them in a hurry.

" Hi Tano," Says Genji.

" Tano, what brings you to the farm?" Asked Ken.

Tano's manner of carrying himself in front of them made Demeter feel strange. His expression was dark, stressed, and concerned. " Ken, something is wrong," said Tano, whispering. This alerted Ken and even Genji.

" What happened?" Asked Ken, concerned.

" Some of the members were found dead in front of the main entrance. Both of their necks were slashed."

Genji turned his way to Ken. The man's eyes were at a loss for words—he had no questions about what or who had caused this. Ken entered fight mode and moved away from his Kimono to reveal the katana on his side.

" Grab the other members and meet me at the front before anyone else finds the bodies," Ken demanded." We don't want this to be heard."

" Got it, sir!" Said Tano as he quickly walked off.

Ken prepares to exit the farm; new priorities are now at stake. Genji has no sight of what will happen but urges himself to help them. " You want me to go with you, father?"

" No!" Ken says aggressively, " Keep helping them with the water situation. I'll be right back." Ken walks off, leaving Genji alone at the farm. Devastation begins in Genji's heart, as he doesn't think his father has trusted him. He understood that Ken was protecting him from some potential killer attack. Genji thought to himself: I'm not a kid anymore.

He wanted to help, even thought about disobeying his father's wishes, and just went ahead along and witnessed this possible murder case. But he respected his father very much and decided not to go, grabbing the bucket and walking off to the lake.

—

Genji heads to the lake, walking through the small

bridges the village had set up to look at the view of it. The water inside was clear like day, reflecting the beautiful motion of the waves as the moon shone brightly toward it. After walking through the bridge, Genji grabs the bucket, kneeling as he gets water into it, one by one. After almost filling up the bucket, he notices strangers in the background with horses coming around the village, fast and urgent. This sparked Genji's attention about what was happening, but without anything else going on straight after, he brushed it off and continued getting the bucket full of water. More people in horses started appearing rapidly, counting six or more people. Genji isn't bothered by it and ignores it as he fills the bucket.

A loud, tragic scream occurs suddenly as a vicious bomb erupts in the village, making Genji drop the bucket and spill the water on the ground. More screaming begins to appear as people from afar start to run for their lives. A concerned, scared boy becomes alert, ready-for-battle man as Genji draws his katana and sprints back to the main center of Koawa.

Genji entered the center, seeing something he had never seen before. Some of the buildings had been destroyed, burning in deep flames, and people were getting killed; the vendors from the festival are now a pile of ashes, and the hosts are on the floor; dead—necks have been cut. People were getting killed and slaughtered. Certain people were running, but some were caught by another samurai whom Genji had never recognized. Genji quickly realizes that another clan is attacking them.

With his father on his mind, Genji quickly begins to look for him. He tries his hardest, but Ken Sato is nowhere to be seen. Out of nowhere, Genji gets shoved. He is on the ground, confused about what just happened. He sees the person who pushed him, a civilian who is now dead. He sees a samurai looking down at him, cleaning the blood off their katana. Genji gets frightened and has no plans for what to do. Without hesitation, he gets up and runs as the samurai chases him.

The samurai sees Genji heading to the dojo and begins to follow him. Genji is nowhere to be seen as the samurai enters the Majo Clan Dojo. They look around, but still, with no trace of Genji. They suddenly get kicked off their feet. Genji, appearing from the shadows in the dojo and carrying his katana, begins to go in his stance. The samurai, getting up from the kick, sees Genji in his stance, holding his katana with aggressive force and rage.

"Who are you? Where is my father?" Genji asks aggressively. The samurai doesn't respond to his question but stands there.

"I guess I'm going to have to beat the answer out of you." Genji then rushes at the samurai. The samurai blocks Genji's katana with theirs, locking eyes as both of their katanas push against each other. They release off from each other and go back, clashing again. Genji goes for another blow, but the samurai effortlessly blocks him. They exchange hits, and the samurai cuts Genji. Without a thought, Genji gets a hit on the samurai, slicing his stomach. Genji goes from behind, stabbing the samurai in the back, hearing them scream in pain. Genji pushes the katana more into the back, and the samurai falls onto the ground, dead.

Genji breathes heavily, taking his katana out of the body. Someone claps in the background. Genji hears it, turns to his right, and sees someone standing before the entrance.

"Not bad for an outsider. I'm guessing Ken taught you well." The stranger walks forward, revealing himself. Genji settles into a defensive stance.

"Who are you? Where is my father, Ken Sato?" asks Genji.

"My name is Takashi. I was going to ask you the same thing." Takashi steps on the mat. Genji and Takashi walk in circles across the mat, staring at each other intensely, not breaking eye contact.

"You better tell me where he is, or I'll kill you," Genji demands viciously.

Takashi doesn't take Genji seriously, and he laughs slightly. "Oh, kid. Genji, is it?" Takashi asked, " Ken and I have some personal things to discuss. I would love to play this little game with you, but I don't have time for child's play."

"I am not a child," Genji said.

"That's exactly what you are, a child who thinks he can be something he's not," Takashi replied to Genji's comment. "Do you know what you're fighting for, kid? I don't know what Ken has put in your head, but you don't know the full story of this annoying little village."

Genji doesn't buy Takshi's comments. He still stands in his position, not moving a muscle. He says, "I hope you fight better than you can talk!" And instinctively rushes to Takashi at full speed, not stopping.

" Stop!" Someone says, making Genji stop in his tracks. Both Genji and Takashi turn their heads and look at the front entrance. They see Ken as entirely okay with his katana, which is already drawn.

"Father, you're okay!" Genji says in relief.

"Ken, I'm happy you can join us," Takashi uttered.

Ken walks forward, thoroughly inside the dojo, a few feet from the mat. "Leave him alone, Takashi," Ken demands. " This has nothing to do with him."

"I don't care; this outcast is in my way," Takashi replies.

"You better watch your fucking mouth!" says Genji

aggressively. " You're talking to the leader of the next generation of The Majo Clan. So you better mind your matters."

" You are no real civilian in Koawa; Genji and Sato is not even your real name," Takashi says. "You were only adopted by the village, but I was born in it and raised in it. But I didn't see the true colors of this place until it was too late."

" The only true colors that appeared were your true intentions ever since our master crowned me the leader of The Majo Clan. And then you went against us and rebelled." Ken interrupted Takashi.

"I only went against you because I saw something more, a revolution of the youth of Samurai," Takashi walked forward to Ken, now facing him dead on as he was now two feet away.

"You only saw war and dictatorship," Ken says as he yells. His tone was fierce, echoing the dojo. "You wanted to turn young, great warriors into blood-lusting, unremorseful samurai. You never cared about being a protector, a leader, a role model to the youth. All you cared about was being a ruler with no morals. We have one Samurai code, and you only want to follow your own."

"There's only one samurai code that everyone must follow: mine. So be it if I must kill every Majo Clan member, including you." Takashi draws his katana, hinting that he's ready for battle. Ken also draws his katana, and both drop into their stances.

"Genji, go. NOW!" yells Ken. Ken and Takashi begin to fight. Genji stands there, watching them both go at it. Ken and Takashi's katanas connect, and they share blows.

Takashi surprises Ken, slicing his right arm and leaving a nasty cut. Takashi kicks Ken off his feet, and Genji angrily sees and screams. Genji draws his katana and rushes after Takashi. Genji tries to hit Takashi, but Takashi dodges, manhandling Genji as he puts him on the ground. Genji tries to get up, but Takashi walks up to Genji and knocks him out by kicking him in the face.

—

Everything is black until Genji suddenly wakes up. His head is still hurting, and his vision is still a bit blurry. As he gains consciousness and vision, he sees that Takashi is gone. Genji gets up to look outside; everything in Koawa is destroyed, bodies and blood everywhere, and some people are severely injured. Genji is devastated and turns around to see something he never wished to see. Ken Sato, with a katana wedged in his back. Genji quickly goes to Ken, panicking with tears running down his face.

Genji takes the katana from Ken's back, catching his father's body as it collapses.

Genji held his father in his arms, hoping for him to wake up, but Genji knew that Ken was gone. Someone comes into the dojo, revealing it to be Tano. He comes to see Genji holding Ken's dead body in his arms as Genji bursts into tears. Tano and Genji look at each other in sorrow. Tano falls to his knees, trying to hold in the tears. Genji holds Ken's body tighter, knowing this is the last time he will hug his father.

RAINTOKU, SEVEN YEARS LATER

S o, this is the night where all hell breaks loose—seven years of planning, scouting, and training for this moment. Nothing can interrupt this now. The rain falls, and the water drops, hitting the grass. I walk through the dark woods; the ground squinches with each step. The darkness is now my ally, as I am in my samurai attire—all black, my face is unseen, and I am wearing my oni mempo dark mask. As I kept walking, almost out of the woods, I saw something that caught my eye: a picture that was nailed to a random tree. I walk forward to look at it, taking it out from the tree, and this isn't just any sign, it's a wanted poster. **RONIN WANTED!** This is what the headline said in bold text. I guess they're looking for me, that's cute—I'm looking for them, and now—I've found them.

I stepped out of the woods and walked down to the entrance of the main central city, Raintoku. I saw rainfall in the dark, cold, and lifeless city of corruption, which people call Raintoku. I remember this place being lovely, a city of saints. People go and find jobs, live in houses—and have an everyday life. Now, that all has been taken away. The clouds appeared gloomy, with no vehicles in sight, as the roads were completely blocked off. A foul stench emanated from the city.

Hundreds of samurai men observe every corner and monitor pedestrians walking through the streets. This place is flooded with samurai men, known as the infamous Rudo Clan. But no one to guard the entrance. They are more worried about people leaving the city rather than breaking in. I sneak into the city, crouching down as I'm in the shadows, observing the streets. The smell in this place is devastating. Well, I guess a corrupted city run by a corrupted man doesn't smell good. It doesn't matter; I'm used to it. The plan stays the same—no different. Now, when the right time comes, I will strike.

Alert, Alert, Alert. A loud alarm goes off and echoes around the city. As I am still in the shadows of the alleyway, I'm seeing how these people react to the alarm. They all gasped and scattered away from the center of Raintoku like ants.

"You hear that alarm, everyone," one of the armed samurai men shouts with the hateful intent to strike fear into the civilians. "Return to your homes, and don't come out past curfew. You know what happens if you do."

Just as I thought this city couldn't get worse, these poor people have a curfew. I saw the fear in their eyes once the clock hit a specific time, and they all ran out like animals. It doesn't surprise me that maybe someone tried to escape or go out past curfew and didn't come out alive.

The whole area is empty and quiet. All I heard was the giant footsteps of the Samurai. The samurai men stand on every corner of the city, guarding the areas and ensuring everything is how it should be. This is just an ordinary night for them. Same routine, different day. That's okay. I know your moves and your little routine. I know where you are, and you don't know where I am, I say let's keep it that way.

"Everything is clear, sir; everyone is in their homes," says one of the men, talking into a mic built into their suit.

They were standing in front of the alley I was in, talking to one of their partners on the mic. This is my time, my moment.

But, I can't go out loud and dumb—Not yet. I must be sneaky, quiet, like a mouse. I need to be silent, but deadly.

I crouch, slowing down as I walk toward the samurai, still standing in the same position. My breathing becomes low, but I am not trying to give up my position. I look for any object that might be in my way as I keep walking, avoiding making any noise. And there I was, behind the man who doesn't even know tonight will be his last. If you feel bad, don't! My people didn't know it would be their last seven years ago. I'm just showing these no-good pieces of shit how it feels to have your life taken away so quickly. I sure hope your men and your family remember you. I grabbed the samurai man, covering his mouth as he tried to get out of my chokehold. I was choking his neck with my forearm, he was unable to escape. After when I found the right moment, I snapped his neck, and then I took his body into the shadows with me.

One down, a hundred more to go. I went to another side of the alley, looking over more of the samurai men in their positions. Something came into my head: I will be here all night if I keep doing this stealth technique. I can't keep this up; I must get from here to there. The tallest building of Raintoku, from what I heard—these people call it The Tower of Rudo. The tower was black, with red light moving around it, and the windows were also tinted red. From what it looks like here, it will take hours to get there. But in reality, it will only take twenty minutes if I run as fast as I can.

I need to do this loud and dumb. So, the first step will be to create a diversion that will bring them all together in one place. I look around this alley to find something to create a big diversion. It caught my eye: an all-black motorcycle parked on the side of the alley. Perfect, this will do.

I went toward the motorcycle, grabbed it, and held it to the center when it tilted to the wall before. On my lucky night, the key to the motorcycle was still in the ignition. Now, it's time to cause some trouble. I turned the key sideways, turning it on. The light beam on the front lit up bright, as the engine was loud. You could hear this from every street corner. Now, I have all of their full attention. I rubbed on both of the handles, preparing for the worst. Then, I release—seeing the motorcycle go out of the alley at full speed, crashing into a light pole. The light pole falls, breaking it and causing the area to be darker.

I saw all the samurai men walking to the middle of the alley, checking out what had just happened. My plan is coming to fruition. " Who there? Show yourself?" one of the samurai men demanded aggressively. Well, all you had to do was ask. Because, once again, the darkness was my ally.

I aggressively run out of the shadow of the alley, coming in full speed. I started attacking the samurai men, catching them off guard. I begin to slice each of them with my katana as I draw it open, cutting their stomachs open and hearing the screams as blood pours out. One of the samurai men lunged at me, but I started to block the attack with my katana and instantly sliced the samurai man's arm in half, leaving the man in pain and screaming in agony while blood was spiraling out of their open wounded arm.

I stop in my tracks, hearing three angry, screaming people coming my way. I put away my katana, and as the other samurai come closer, without hesitation, grabbing from my side, I throw three small knives at them. The knives jammed through their skull, killing them instantly while they dropped down to the ground like flies.

Why don't you look at that? Another samurai man is trying to attack from behind. I dodged, punching him in the gut, unleashing my katana, and slicing the samurai man's head off. The head was way up in the sky, and the body was already on the ground. The head begins to come back down; I do a spinning kick to hit the head in another direction, separating the head from its body. There's no time to waste. I need to get to that tower before anything else happens. I started to sprint, but through the roads, not carrying who would see me anymore, the tower was the only thing on my mind.

Alert, Alert, Alert. A loud alarm alerts the entire city. An unfamiliar voice begins to speak through an intercom through the entire city.

"Attention Rudo Clan members and everyone in Raintoku. The city is in full lockdown; we have an intruder. Make sure to stay in your homes until the lockdown is over, and members, find the intruder and bring their head to Sir Takashi's desk; thank you!"

Damn! Everyone knows my presence. It doesn't matter, let them all come. I'll take them all out by ease, and then I'll go and kill their beloved boss. I'm coming for you, Takashi, you fucking coward. You can stay in your little office as long as you want, sending your men to do your dirty work. But when you find out that all of them are flat out on the ground, lifeless, you will know I'm not fucking around. I'm coming for blood, for vengeance, for justice.

In the distance, I see hundreds of Rudo Clan members running toward me rapidly out of the main building. This doesn't affect me; I take out my katana and rush toward them faster and more confidently. I effortlessly stand my ground as we all run into each other. I block their hits, cutting off their limbs and heads and penetrating their stomachs with my katana. Blood is splattered everywhere. I run through them with unimaginable strength, hearing their screams, pain, and agony but having no remorse. They had no remorse when they killed my people. Fuck their lives, like I said—I'm coming for blood.

I continue to fight off all the clan members effortlessly. After I was done wiping the floor with these folks, The remaining members gathered in a circle, trapping me in the middle. I once again stand my ground, ready to go to war again. There's nothing that these men can do to stop me. Do they think they're dangerous? I have nothing to lose anymore—I'm the dangerous one.

I'm not stuck in Raintoku with them; they're stuck in Raintoku with me!

"STOP!" Someone yelled in the background; I didn't see who said it as all the members were in a circle around me. "That's enough; let the boy through," says the person. The remaining Rudo members all stood back behind me, revealing who it was that was talking. Goddamn Takashi, walking in front of me, wearing an all-black silk suit. Two other people behind him.

This doesn't surprise me at all. I stay sharp, eyes up, and don't let my guard down.

"My men are the most trained samurai in all of Japan. And for you to take them all down is almost impressive," says Takashi. "Majo Clan taught you well...Genji Sato."

"So, you remember me?" I asked. I take off my mask, revealing my face.

"Of course, how could I forget such a face?" Takashi said to me.

"So, you also know why I'm here," I added. Takashi chuckles, thinking this is a fucking game and not taking me seriously.

"The Majo and Rudo Clans have conflicted for years, even before you came around Genji," Takashi says. "Ken and I had unfinished business, so I finished it myself."

His saying made my blood boil and made me tighten my katana. My jaw became tense; I wanted to say many things to this man—but my mind was going one hundred miles per hour; I couldn't think straight. But then, I whispered, "For seven years... I have been waiting for this very moment. You took everything from me. My village, my people, and my father. And for that, I'm going to make you pay," I say as I stare into Takashi's eyes like a hawk, not breaking any eye contact.

"Your father? Your village?" says Takashi, laughing hysterically. "You think that Ken loved you? You were nothing but an outsider. Ken only took you in to fill the hole his dead family left in his heart."

Anything that comes out of his mouth is a lie. How could he say that? He's not a man with integrity.

"He used you, but you were too blind and stupid to realize that," Takashi told me, "You don't belong here; you never did."

The rage gripped me, and every ounce of my temper began to spark. Enough of this, I didn't come here to talk. I raise my katana toward Takashi's face. "I will make you eat those words as I cut them out of your fucking throat..."

"I would love to see you try," says Takashi confidently.

Both of us intensely stare down at each other. Having waited years, I finally get the urge to begin what I've been wanting. I scream in rage and rush toward Takashi. Takashi isn't fazed and stands still. That's alright; I'm not fazed either. I swing my katana at Takashi, but Takashi effortlessly dodges the blow.

His dodge surprised me. No matter, I continued to attack Takashi. I kept swinging my katana, throwing blows left and right. The rain still fell hard, while the Rudo clan members were watching us. I missed these blows continuously. How can this be? What am I doing wrong? Am I telegraphing my hits? The thought angered me, but Takashi finds this amusing.

"Is that all you've got?" Takashi said behind me. You haven't seen anything yet, Takashi; just wait.

I then swing my katana once again, but he grabs me by my arm and throws me on the ground hard., which causes me to drop my katana.

"It seems like Ken didn't teach you very well. You fucking amateur...and you're supposed to be a samurai," says Takashi as he laughs.

I will show you a fucking amateur. I get up, a little hurt by getting slammed on the ground, but that didn't stop me one bit. I then raised both of hands up, making them into fists. This amused Takashi, I looked him in the eye as he smiled. " Now we talkin," Takashi said. I run in to hit blows, but I miss a few shots. I went ahead and went for a jab. But then, Takashi stops it by parrying it away. Takashi starts to fight back. Punching me in the ribs, face, and stomach. This can't be happening, I was unable to withstand Takashi's power, and I was kicked off my feet and fell to the ground once again. I get up, not giving up—I still have more fight in me. But Takashi puts me back on the ground. He punches me constantly. I started to feel dizzy, as I couldn't feel the pain anymore.

I struggled to get up, coughing up blood and grunting in pain. This couldn't be happening, It can't end like this—not now. I needed this, to avenge everyone. If I lose tonight, then they all died for nothing. I did not come this far to die now. As a samurai, you are supposed to accept death, as a true warrior should. But I'm no samurai, not anymore—Only a ronin.

"It's a shame, I was hoping for a better fight," says Takashi. He kneels in front of me and grabs me by the neck. "But your anger clouds your judgment." I began to look at Takashi with blood dripping down my face. "You will always be an outcast and an outsider. Believe what you want, but you were never a true samurai, and Ken was never your father," Takashi then gets up and walks away from me, leaving me on my knees in defeat.

"And you were never a protector, that's why Ken was the chosen one and not you," I uttered at him, saying my last words. If I'm going to die, then I can't leave without saying the truth. "That's why you killed him? Because of jealousy? You are a pathetic man who thinks he's a god, a ruler, and a warrior. While a true warrior and a true leader doesn't act on jealousy."

Before I could say more, Takashi walked up to me and viciously kneed me in the face, making me go down again. I was out; my vision became a blur. All the sounds, scents, and sights were obsolete. This was it; I was defeated. How can I be so blind, so reckless? I failed my father, I failed my people, I failed myself. All those years of grief, mourning, and training, and for what? Dieing like this.

The only thing I heard before completely blacking out was Takashi demanding his men.

"Grab the body and throw it in the lake."

CHAPTER 2

ECHOES OF DESTINY

The neighborhood of Weeksville in Brooklyn, at night. The streetlights are bright, and the environment is as quiet as a mouse. A young boy runs in the neighborhood toward a small home. He stops in his tracks to catch his breath. The boy looks behind him as if he assumes someone is chasing him. One of his eyes is swollen, and his shirt is slightly ripped. He walks inside a house, which so happens to be his home. He stops to see his mother standing before him, waiting at the front door, her expression upset.

"Harold Davis! Where have you been? You were supposed to be home from the park an hour ago..." says Destiny Davis

"I'm sorry, momma, I was playing with my friends, and I just forgot to come home, lost track of time," Harold responds defensively.

The mother notices a big bruise on Harold's eye, and her face turns into concern. "What happened to your eye?"

"I fell from the monkey bars." "The monkey bars?"

"Yes."

"It doesn't look like it to me, don't lie to me, Harold..."

"Okay, okay, I'll tell you the truth...my friends and I were playing, and some kids came to the park and started picking on this kid who was minding his own business. I saw it, got mad, and went and told them to stop. One of the kids punched me, so I hit them back; Then we all were just fighting. Then the cops came, and we all panicked and ran; so I came home."

Destiny stays silent, thinking what to say to Harold. Controlling her frustration, She breathes deeply, closes her eyes, then opening them back up.

"Okay, go to the kitchen and get an ice bag to put on your eye," says the mother.

"Okay, Momma."

—

Hours go by, and Harold and his mother sit in the dining room eating dinner. In the background, a door opens.

"I'm home everyone!" the man says as he walks into the front door.

"Isaiah, please get in here!" Destiny shouts.

Isaiah comes in with a concern, kissing Destiny's forehead. "Hey, what's up? Harold, what happened to your eye?"

"Harold got into a fight at the park earlier. Some kids were picking on a boy then Harold defended him, and this happened."

"What was I supposed to do, just stand there and watch that boy get bullied?" says Harold defensively. "I'm sorry for fighting, but I couldn't just let him get picked on like that. I'd rather have this black eye knowing that I helped that kid when he needed it. Please don't be mad at me Dad..."

"I'm not mad at you, Harold. If anything, I'm proud of

you," says, Isaiah. His concern fades away as he comforts Harold.

"Wait really? You're not mad?"

"No, that was very brave of you to stick up for that kid, that was the right thing to do," says Isaiah.

Harold smiles in relief and rushes to hug Isaiah.

"Okay now, go and get ready for bed," Destiny demands.

"Okay, Mom!" Harold replies.

Harold runs out of the kitchen with excitement. "That boy is something isn't he?" Isaiah adds.

"I'm very happy that he did what he did. But I don't like him fighting a lot, what if something bad happened?"

"Destiny calm down, I'm sure everything was fine, yeah he got a black eye, but that will heal in no time."

"He's only ten, he shouldn't be fighting at this age, he's just a kid."

"Okay, I see what you're saying, but he knows right from wrong. It's not like he fought the kid to fight, it was in self-defense; he was only looking after that little boy. It was only a stupid fight, what worse could have happened?"

—

I woke up startled. What happened? I thought I was dead. My eyes wander around, seeing my katana on the floor near a door. The room was lit up with only one lightbulb. Where the hell am I? I was cramped as I was laying on a small twin bed; it was tiny for a man like me that's six foot and one-ninety pounds. I tried to get up, but a pain in my stomach struck, but I managed. I limped while walking toward the room door. I opened it, and what I saw took me by alarming surprise. I noticed An old man cooking food in a kitchen. It didn't take me too long to realize that I was in a random house. The old man then turned around and noticed me standing in front of the door to the room I was just in.

"Oh, Mr. Sato, you're up!" says the old man, shocked to see me.

"Who the hell are you? Where am I?" I asked defensively.

"Oh, don't worry sir, you're safe. My name is Shiro, Shiro Hamasaki! I found you in a lake underwater in Raintoku. You were badly hurt, so I brought you to my home in Shinano..." Shiro replied.

"Shinano? Why didn't you take me to a hospital?" I asked.

"The hospital was too far, Mr. Sato; I didn't want to leave you there, so my only option was to bring you here. I cleaned you up and fixed your bruises."

I looked down at myself, seeing the badges I had on my body. I guess I was badly hurt. Fuck, now I remembered. I lost, I was beaten. It made me think of the night, where me and Takashi fought. I could've died, and this man saved my life.

" Thank you," I say to him. "How long was I out?"

"Only for a few hours," Shiro says.

I heard a door open coming from the front of the house. Someone came through, causing Shiro and me to look in the direction of the front door. It was a woman coming into the house. I couldn't believe my eyes. I was hurt, but she Was the most beautiful woman I had ever seen. Her hair was rolled up into a little ponytail, and she was wearing a lovely flora Kimono dress.

She noticed me and Shiro in the kitchen, her expression counted as surprised to see me.

"Mr. Sato, this is my daughter, Ai," says Shiro.

"Father! What's going on?" Ai asked, the tone of her voice in all concern.

"It's okay, sweetheart. Mr. Sato was in trouble, and he's going to stay for a while until he's better." Shiro replied to her.

I interrupted him because my staying here was not a part of the plan, well, not mine, at least. "Look mister, I appreciate you helping me, but I can't stay here. There's a vital mission I must seek." I proceeded to walk away, heading toward the front door of the house, but the pain and bruises were too much for me; I suddenly collapsed, falling onto the ground. I grunt in pain, now unable to get up.

Shiro comes over to my rescue and kneels to get to my level. "Mr. Sato, you cannot do anything right now. You are badly hurt...please return to the room and lie down." Shiro says,

I, lying on the ground in disappointment, accept my injuries. I got up from the ground, with Shiro's assistance by helping me. I stared at both Shiro and Ai; the room was nothing but silent. I obeyed Shiro's request and began to limp back to the room and slowly shut the door behind me.

———

I was back in the room. The night was still in play. I didn't know the time; I had so many things in my head going around at once—I couldn't think straight. But the moon looked so beautiful, as the window was open and it was shining into the room. The night's sky was something like an old painting, full of color against the inky, black abyss. The stars in the sky were twinkling like diamonds. While the outside world looked lovely, my world was hell. I was defeated and embarrassed.

I fell down to my knees in the bedroom with the lights off. I looked down at my katana as the moonlight shone down at it. I had a lump in my throat and was blinking away the tears. **Father, if you're hearing me right now, I'm sorry...I should be dead, I shouldn't be here. I don't know if this means something or if God is giving me a second chance, But why me?** I tighten around my katana, with one spec of tears beginning to fall on the blade, seeing my reflection. **After all these years, they took everything away from us...they took you away from me. I tried so hard, but I failed. My emotions got the best of me, and if you were here, I feel like you'd see me as a fool.** I grabbed the katana, holding it in the light. **I miss you so much, Father...I'm so sorry I failed you. I don't deserve to be alive.**

I draw my katana and close my eyes. **I don't deserve this**

second chance. I slowly position my katana toward my stomach. I breathe heavily while slowly pulling my katana closer to myself. I nearly impale myself as my mind races, hating myself for all my faults and wanting everything to end. **"FOCUS!"** a voice loudly whispers in my head. I stopped, startled by the voice. I could feel a presence; I opened my eyes. **Father?**

I dropped the katana on the ground and fell on my back. I look up at the ceiling and close my eyes to try to hear my father's voice again. **Please talk to me, father. What do you want me to do?** I sit there, waiting for an answer. Nothing, I don't hear anything anymore.

—

A scream occurs outside the room that wakes Harold up. Harold quickly gets up from his bed and rushes out of the door. He goes to the living room and sees three angry men in the living room with his parents. Two pins Destiny down, while another one of them aims their gun at Isaiah. Harold is in disbelief at what's happening; Destiny is in tears, begging them to let them go and leave.

One of them notices Harold in the living room, staring, "Hey, get the fuck on the ground Now!" One of the robbers shouts at Harold with a demanding tone. Without hesitation, Harold gets down on the ground.

"Now, I'm not going ask you again, Isaiah, where's my fucking money?" Said one of the robbers.

"Look, man, I already told you I don't have it right now. Please just give me a couple more weeks..." Isaiah said, scared.

"We already gave you a whole month nigga. Don't bullshit me!"

"I promise I'm not...just please let my family go," Isaiah begs.

The robber gets frustrated, then looks at one of his companions and directs them to Harold. One of them

rushes to Harold, aggressively picks him up, and points the gun at his head. Destiny screams, cries, and yells.

"Please! Don't do this, I will get you your money, okay I'm sorry," Isaiah begs with tears running down his face. The robber doesn't feel remorse for what they're doing.

"It's too late now bro, you fucked up..." says the robber. He looks at one of the companions and nods at them. They nod back, take one step back, and shoot Destiny in the head, her body falling to the ground.

"MOMMA!" Harold screams.

Isaiah falls on his knees as he begs them to stop. Harold's tears and sadness turn into rage, and he suddenly turns to grab the gun away from the robber. He succeeds and shoots both the robbers in the head. The power of the shots makes Harold fall on his back. Isaiah tackles the last robber to the ground and fights him.

The robber gets the upper hand and quickly shoots Isaiah in the stomach, making him fall onto the ground. The robber looks at Harold and tries to get up, but Harold shoots him before he can move.

Harold stands in shock, his whole body shaking. He slowly walks to his father who is still alive but is losing a lot of blood. Harold drops the gun and holds onto Isaiah. He sobs as he holds Isaiah's hand. Isaiah has trouble speaking, he looks at Harold, raises his hand, and gently touches Harold's face. He takes one good look at his son, knowing this will be the last time he sees him; then his eyes roll back in his head, and he stops moving.

Harold is devastated and heartbroken. One of his tears falls on Isaiah's forehead. Harold suddenly hears sirens coming. He gets startled and quickly rushes toward the window to look.

He sees seven police cars in front of the house and hears more coming. Harold panics, he stops to look at all the bodies on the floor. Without any hesitation, Harold runs to the back of the house, gets outside, climbs the gates, and quickly leaves the area.

Even when he's far away, Harold does not stop running. When he finally has no more energy to run, he stops in his tracks. He collapses on the ground and starts to cry once again. Harold balls up on the ground and lies in sorrow.

CHAPTER 3

THE OUTSIDER

One day later, Harold walks around Brooklyn at night. Everything has come crashing down into the young boy's life. Tired, starving, and desperate for some kind of sustenance. He asks individuals for money, but nobody acknowledges him. He thinks about walking back home but is afraid to do so.

His stomach growls, desperate for food. He looks around to see if there are any stores nearby. Luckily, Harold sees a local grocery store. A smile comes out, a smile that hasn't been shown ever since the home invasion. He goes into the grocery store, overwhelmed by his surroundings. Individuals look at him with concern and confusion. Harold knows this but doesn't pay attention.

Harold walks around every food aisle there is, staring at all the food there. Even though he is hungry, he is very picky about choosing the right food. After minutes of looking, he finds a snack he remembers his mom getting him all the time. He grabs it and proceeds to leave, but he stops, remembering that he has no money to pay for the snack. Harold looks around the store and sees seven different store employees walking around. He gets an idea that is risky, but it's the only option.

He proceeds to walk toward the cash register, next in line. Without hesitation, he quickly runs out of the grocery store, employees yelling for someone to stop him. Harold runs as far as he can until he doesn't see the store anymore. After minutes of running, Harold comes to a stop, gasping for air, and feeling like throwing up. Harold looks around his surroundings to see if anyone followed him, but he is in the clear. Harold is in disbelief at what he did but is relieved that he succeeded. He runs to a dark alley and begins to eat the snacks that he took from the store.

He hears footsteps coming from the back of the alley. He stops eating, concerned about who is coming. Three young boys walk out of the shadows talking and laughing. Harold recognizes the three, as he had gotten into a fight with them a couple of days before the home invasion. Before Harold can try to hide, one of them notices him.

"Hey, who's that?" says one of the kids. "Wait a minute...Harold Davis? No fucking way, this boy became homeless."

The three boys begin to laugh at Harold. After everything he and the boys went through on that fateful day, the desperation comes through, and he asks the boys for help.

"Please guys I need help, I have nowhere to go, is it okay if I use one of you guy's phones?" says Harold.

"Oh my god, sure dude. You guys pick him up and I'll grab my phone."

The two kids proceeded to help Harold as he was sitting on the floor. As soon as Harold got up, one of the kids suddenly punched Harold hard, Causing Harold to fall once again in pain.

"Fuck you, little punk," says one of the kids, angrily.

The two kids once again grab Harold to make him stand up. Harold still grunts in pain after the vicious punch.

"This is what you get for giving me a black eye."

The kid again punches Harold till he falls to the ground. After the kids proceed to punch, kick, and stomp on Harold, he becomes unresponsive, with his eyes now swollen shut.

"HEY!"An angry voice yells from the distance. The three boys look forward, and they see a man standing in front of them.

"Step away from the boy, NOW!" says the man. "What is it to you, old man?"

The man then walks forward, revealing himself, as a Japanese man.

"Go home...I won't ask again..." The man then pulls out a large knife from his sleeve. The three kids see and immediately, without no hesitation, run away to where they came from. The man then looks at Harold who is in bad condition. He goes up to Harold, looks at him, and sees his injuries.

"Are you okay?" says the man. Harold doesn't respond. The man fears that Harold might be dead, but he is still breathing. The man looks at his surroundings to see if anyone is looking in his direction. The man gently picks up Harold and walks away from the alley.

—

Harold is now awake after hours of being unconscious. He wakes up in a room that he's not familiar with. While he is still in a bit of pain, Harold gets up from the bed and starts to walk around the room.

Harold quickly looks out the window and sees the view of everything. Harold is overwhelmed by the view he is looking at when suddenly someone gets out of the bathroom. Harold gets startled and quickly turns to see the man. They both stop to look at each other.

"Don't worry, I'm not going to hurt you."

"Who are you?" asks Harold, scared.

"My name is Ken, Ken Sato. We're in a hotel room that I'm staying at." Harold is scared, and he proceeds to walk further away from Ken.

"Are you going to hurt me?"

"No of course not, you're safe I promise you. When I walked back here, I saw you getting hurt by those kids. They were going to kill you, so I stopped them, and brought you back here."

Harold lowers his guard after hearing Ken.

"Okay, now what's your name? And where do you live so I can take you back home?" says Ken.

After hearing that, Harold immediately starts crying. Ken gets confused about Harold's reaction..

"What's wrong?" Ken asks in concern.

"I don't have a home anymore..."

"What do you mean? Where are your parents?"

Harold doesn't say anything, just proceeds to cry more.

"Kid, I have to know where your parents are so that I can take you to them."

"You can't..."

"Why can't I?"

"Because they're dead. They died last night, I saw them die...I ran away from home because I shot the people who killed them, and I'm scared that the police will put me away forever. I just feel like everything is my fault. I just want my mom and dad to come back to me..." Harold cries again. Ken feels sympathy for Harold but doesn't say anything after that.

Ken walks toward Harold to comfort him. "What's your name kid?"

"Harold."

"And how old are you?"

"Ten."

"Okay. Believe it or not, I know what you're going through right now, but no kid your age should have to go through that and I'm sorry."

Harold then wipes the tears off his face.

"So, here's what we're going to do, I'll give you a choice. One, we can go to the police, and you tell them everything you told me. They will keep you and help find somewhere for you to go. Or two, you can come back home with me to Japan. I have a village there named Koawa.

There, I will take care of you and make sure that you are safe," Ken says.

Both of them are silent as Harold looks up at Ken. His concern and skepticism disappear as he puts his full trust in Ken.

"You promise you will keep me safe?" asks Harold.

"You have my word, Harold."

As Ken speaks, Harold's face changes. Before, he was scared and hopeless. Now, Harold smiles a little as he begins to trust Ken.

—

The sunlight shines bright in the room as I sit on the bed lying down. I didn't sleep at all last night. Everything that happened before, my mind had too much stuff for me to have a good night's sleep. Someone knocks at the door, softly. " Come in," I say. It was Ai, as she came into the room.

"Good morning, Mr. Sato, I hope I'm not bothering you," says Ai. "Good morning, no, you're not bothering me, and please call me Genji," I say.

"Sorry, I've made some breakfast, so whenever you're ready, you can come in the kitchen and eat," says Ai. She then leaves the room, leaving me alone. I could go for something to eat.

After she mentioned breakfast, my stomach started to rumble. I touched my stomach, not knowing how long it's been since I've eaten a proper meal.

I walk out of the door, seeing Ai and Shiro at the dinner table eating breakfast. We all lock eyes. I walked toward the kitchen table and sat where the food was placed. I don't say a word to either of them and just begin to eat the food.

"How are you feeling?" asks Shiro.

"Fine, still trying to process everything that happened," I replied to him.

"I know it must be a lot for you right now. I know you samurai men must have a lot going on in your mind."

" I'm no samurai," I uttered. " Not anymore."

" What happened?" Shiro asked.

"I'd rather not get into it right now," I say." I just wanted to say thank you for letting me stay here and saving my life. I don't know if I would still be here if it weren't for you."

"Oh, of course, Mr. Sato." Shiro said.

"Please, call me Genji." I told him.

"Sorry, of course, Genji."

We all remained silent and continued eating. After a few bites, I was amazed at the meal, and my face began to light up.

"This meal is really good, thank you...I don't know the last time I had a proper meal."

"I'm glad you like it," says Ai. "So... Genji, what were you doing in Raintoku?" she added.

"AI!" Shiro yells at her.

"What, Father? If he's going to be staying with us, we have to know his intentions with the Rudo Clan," Ai said.

"That is not our business to ask him that!"

"This is our home. It is our business!"

"She's right," I say to both of them. Because she was. Shiro saved my life, and now I'm here in their home.

"You both deserve to know," I said. "I'm on a very personal mission to stop Takashi Kuri, the dangerous man who runs the

Rudo Clan. That's why I was there...to stop all of them, but I failed."

"Is it because of what happened in Koawa?" Ai asked

"Yes, I don't want to talk about that, but...I will make them pay." I say, "I'm surprised you knew about that."

"Your father was a great man, Genji, a great samurai. He helped everyone in need in every town, village, and city. So, when we heard about it, we were devastated," said Shiro.

My father was a great man and a great samurai. I remember the stories people told me back in Koawa when I was little about my father being a savior to everyone. He helped the ones in need. He not only helped people in Koawa; he also helped all of the towns and villages without clans protecting them. I remember when I last talked to him, before the ambushed. He told me the purpose he had for the group and him. **As the protectors, we have the purpose to help the ones who can't help themselves and to fight for the ones who can't fight back themselves.**

"Okay well, I have to go to work. Genji, whenever you're ready to shower, I left my old kimono in the guest bathroom for you, hopefully, it fits you." Shiro said as he got up.

"Thank you, Shiro." I said to him.

"Ah, of course." Shiro kisses Ai on the forehead. "Have a good day, sweetheart. Make sure to keep him company."

Shiro left the kitchen. Ai and I sat and finished our oatmeal. When I was done, I grabbed my bowl and headed to the kitchen sink.

"Oh, don't worry about that; I'll take care of it. I always wash the dishes." Ai told me.

"Oh no, don't worry. It's fine. I can put away my plate. As a matter of fact, do you want me to take yours?" I asked her.

Her faced stood still after my suggestion, I caught it and raised my concern. "What's wrong?"I asked.

"Oh, nothing." Ai handed me the plate, and I went to put the dishes in the sink and proceeded to wash all of the dishes.

—

Later in the day, I decided to take a shower in the guest bathroom they had in their home. I get out and begin to dry myself off.

After a few moments of drying myself off, I can feel another presence near me. It was strange, almost like I was being watched. Suddenly I turned my back, looking in the direction of the bathroom door, and I slightly saw Ai watching me. She quickly ran off, and hearing her footsteps going away I heard a door slam. I smiled slightly, I was flattered by how she was kinda checking me out. But I didn't pay more attention to it. When I got done drying off and tying my hair into a ponytail, I then went and put on the old kimono that Shiro left for me. It was an ordinary black with white stripes. I put it on, looking at myself in the mirror. It does fit actually. I haven't worn a Kimono for a while. I looked good, smiling at myself.

—

" Wake up, Harold," Said Ken, " We're here."

Harold wakes up from his nap on the plane. He's feeling tired, but as he looks around, and assumes that they made it to their destination.

"We're here already?"

"It was a fourteen-hour flight."

"Is that a long time?"

"For the most part, yes."

"Oh, well it felt like five minutes."

"Well, you were sleeping half of the time, so it flew by."

As everyone gets off the plane, Ken and Harold proceed to walk into the airport looking for the exit, Harold is a bit excited about this new journey in life. He still feels a bit unsure about Ken's backstory.

"I have a question."

"I have an answer."

"What do you do exactly?"

"I'll tell you all about it once we arrive at our destination." "Where's that at?"

"Back at my village, Koawa."

"What's a village? Is it like a farm? Do people live there? Do animals live there?

"Okay, Harold look... I know all of this is new to you and you have a lot of questions, and I will happily answer them all for you. But right now, we have to get to Koawa and get everything sorted out with you. So please, save your questions until we get there, okay?"

"Okay..."

They walk out of the airport. Harold looks around and is overwhelmed by everything he sees. Ken sees a taxi, signaling it to stop by waving his hand. Ken and Harold both get inside to go to the village.

"I have another question," says Harold.

"I thought I said no more questions until we get to Koawa."

"I know, I know, but this question is important."

"Okay, what is it?"

"What made you want to leave here and come to Brooklyn, New York exactly?"

"I just wanted to go somewhere new and explore new things. I've stayed in Japan and my village for as long as I can remember. I never really got to explore the other parts of the world, and New York was a place I chose randomly."

"Oh, well I'm glad you did choose New York."

"Yeah, me too...."

—

After hours of driving, they finally arrive at Koawa. Ken and Harold get out of the taxi. Harold takes one good look at the village and is amazed. Koawa is a village of peace. Civilians walk through the village, and the sun shines through peacefully as many kids run and

play. Some civilians play beautiful music, while others
dance.

"Woah, look at this place..."

"It's nice, huh?"

"Yeah! This is where I'm going to be staying?"

"Yes, come on, follow me."

They begin to walk into the village. As they walk,
everyone starts waving at Ken and welcoming him.
Harold looks around at every little thing the village has
to offer. As everyone is happy to see Ken, others
strangely stare at Harold in confusion and concern.
Harold notices this and feels uncomfortable. Certain
people are staring, pointing, and whispering. Their
walking causes attention to everyone, when suddenly
someone stops them in their tracks.

"Ken Sato! Welcome back home."

"Thank you, Tano."

Tano looks down at Harold and looks back up and
Ken, with confusion on his face. "And I see you have
brought a guest."

"Tano, this is Harold, Harold...this is Tano, my
partner."

"Hi, nice to meet you!" Harold puts his hand up to
Tano to shake his hand. Tano sees but does not budge.

"Can me and the members talk to you for a minute
Ken, alone..."

"Oh okay, hold on for a moment." Ken takes Harold
aside to talk with him. "Hey, I need to discuss some
things, so, how about you sit over there at the small
stairs, and I'll be right back."

"How long will you be gone?"

"Hopefully not too long, just wait for me, and don't
get into any trouble okay."

"Okay..."

Harold goes over to the stairs to sit as Ken insisted.

Ken and Tano leave and head over to their dojo. As they arrive, Ken is greeted by more members. They all bow to Ken as a welcome for him.

"Okay, so what is it about?" says Ken.

"When you told me you were going out of town, you didn't say anything about bringing an outsider to our village," says Tano.

After Tano's comment, the rest of the members are surprised, looking at Ken in disbelief. "That outsider has a name, Tano."

"It doesn't matter Ken; you know what happens to an outsider that steps foot in Koawa."

"What's his name?" asks one of the members. "His name is Harold, Harold Davis."

The members look at each other in distress, while Tano faces palms in disappointment. "Ken, this is against the samurai code. Koawa has been a sacred village for generations. This place has rules, and it's up to us as the Majo Clan to follow those rules and protect this village from people who could be a threat to us."

"He's just a kid, Tano! Why are you making him out to be some monster? He's been through a lot, okay? He lost his mother and father, and his home. So, I brought him here to give him a second chance at a new life."

Ken hears laughing coming from outside. He looks and notices Harold playing and laughing with two other kids. Ken is relieved that Harold is already making himself at home.

"I know what you're trying to do Ken...And look, I'm sorry for his loss but, you can't be that boy's father. Even if you tried, you can't heal your broken wounds from your past," says Tano.

"My past has nothing to do with this. As your leader, what I say goes. He's going to stay here, and you all will be treating him with the same respect as you do the others. At the end of the day, he's just a kid and he's human just like the rest of us. Is that understood?"

"Yes sir," says everyone.

"Tano?"

"He will have my respect, sir..."

"Good."

Ken leaves the building and heads over to Harold as he is playing with the other kids.

Harold sees Ken and proceeds to run toward him in all excitement. "It looks like you're making friends already," says Ken.

"Yeah, they're very cool. They showed me this card game called Kruta and it's awesome!"

"Ahh Kruta, haven't played that game in years, I'm glad you're settling in, Harold."

"I am! What were you discussing?" asks Harold.

"Oh, just some work stuff, nothing important. But come on, let me show you where you going to be staying at."

"Okay! Is it your house?"

"Yes, lucky for you, I have an extra room for you to sleep in."

"Okay, cool. I am kind of tired, you know, because of the jet lag and stuff."

"Yeah, don't worry. Once we get you situated, you will be able to go to sleep."

Harold and Ken proceed to leave, heading to Ken's home, where Harold will be sleeping.

—

I exited the bathroom, thinking about what I should do next. After all, I had a lot of time on my hands. I walked inside the living room of their home. Now, looking at it, it was charming. There is nice grey coloring on the walls, and I see the black couch being well put together. I looked forward, and I noticed that they had a backyard. I thought to myself, and think going outside for fresh air wouldn't be so bad.

I stepped foot into the backyard of the house. The outside amazes me as the leaves blow softly in the wind, the sun shines down, and the grass is greener than he can ever imagine, flowing with the wind gracefully. For seven years of my life, I always had darkness in my mind and red in my eyes. For the first time in forever, I felt at peace physically. But what about mentally? I still had internal things I had to face. Doing a small meditation would do the trick. I haven't done this for so long, but it will help.

I sit on top of the stairs, embracing everything nature offers. I close my eyes and start the meditation, breathing in and out to clear my mind.

I begin to wander inside my head, looking back at my thoughts. All the negative, bad things that happened to me started returning. I'm focusing and fighting back all my fears, guilt, and negative thoughts. I remembered things from years ago that I couldn't remember then. I don't know if I chose not to remember it or if my mind did it for me. The negative thoughts began to overpower me, and I was losing focus. But then, I remember the voice of his father's spirit: **FOCUS**.

With all of my will and determination, all the negative thoughts finally faded away, leaving my mind like a speck of dust in the wind. After everything had flown away, I felt free. I couldn't hear the pain or feel it anymore. I heard the birds chirping, the wind flowing through my body, and the grass moving in motion. So this is what it feels like. My mind now being free. I felt great physically, but spiritually, I was now at peace.

—

Takashi is in his dojo training with four other members. Two of them rush toward Takashi to attack, but Takashi counters them and knocks them down. The last two, take their fighting positions. Takashi confidently looks at them, urging them to make the first

move. The two remaining members draw their sparring weapons, preparing for the fight.

"Sir!" says Takashi's assistant, interrupting the spar, which irritates Takashi. "What is the problem? Can't you see that I'm busy?"

"My apologies sir, but we have a major problem."

Takashi stops, telling all four of the members to leave the dojo. "What problem is that?" "When you took down one of the members of the Majo Clan that night and threw him off a bridge...."

"If you think they're going to send more members to come and try to defeat me then you are mistaken, they're not that stupid."

"No, you don't understand, sir; he's not dead."

"What are you talking about?" Takashi asks in disbelief.

"When I was looking at old security footage, I saw the night of when the samurai got thrown and...just look at this."

The security shows Takashi footage of the night when his men threw Genji off the bridge. In the footage, someone goes into the water, grabbing Genji's body out of the lake.

"Who is that?"

"It's a man, sir, I did some scanning and investigation, and it looks like the man's name is Shiro Hamasaki. A sixty-year-old man who lives in Shnano with his only daughter, Ai Hamasaki. That's probably where the samurai is hiding right now."

Takashi is unwilling to accept the realization that Genji is still alive. He begins to doubt himself, his strength, and his will.

"Impossible...am I weak?" "Um, no sir."

"THEN WHY THE FUCK ISN'T GENJI SATO DEAD?" screams Takashi.

"I told you sir; the old man saved him. I promise you, sir, you're not weak, it was just an inconvenience."

"An inconvenience? That wasn't an inconvenience, that was luck."

"Well, what do you want us to do, sir? Genji Sato could be planning his next attack at this very moment."

"That coward won't come back, I know for certain that I broke him, his spirit, and his will. Gather all of the remaining members and gear up. Head to Shnano and bring Genji Sato back here so to me so I can kill him properly this time. And if you all fail to capture him, the price will be far worse than what I'm about to do to Genji Sato himself."

"But sir, what do you want us to do with the people in Shnano?"

"Eliminate them all..."

CHAPTER 4

DARK RECKONING

I was sitting on top of the stairs, now looking at the view of the background. The meditation worked perfectly, as I became familiar with nature. Suddenly, I hear someone opening the doorway behind me. " Good afternoon, Genji," Said Ai, as she walked up behind, getting closer.

" Good afternoon, Ai" I say. " Saying hi would've been way better than staring."

"What are you talking about?" She asked.

"You're very sneaky, but I knew I felt someone watching me as I was drying off in the bathroom earlier." I said as I mentioned her, watching me as I was in the bathroom.

Ai realizes what I was talking about, and she gets embarrassed. "Oh my God Genji, I'm so sorry...I should never have done that."

I then laughed, finding it amusing, but I gave her some slack. "Oh no, it's fine, believe it or not. I'm very flattered," I chuckled. Ai blushes, feeling relieved that I wasn't mad at her.

She then changed the topic to something else: "So, um, what are you doing?"

"Just sitting here, thinking," I replied. " I don't remember the last time I sat immersed in nature; it's peaceful. Shinano is such a beautiful town with a great environment."

Ai proceeds to sit next to me on the benches as we both stare out into the sky with the leaves blowing by.

"Shinano is a wonderful place. I've lived here ever since I was born; I can't imagine living anywhere else," says Ai.

"Your father, I owe a debt to him for saving my life. He's a good man." I say to her, giving her father credit.

"Yeah, he's always willing to help others in need."

"If you don't mind me asking, do you have a mother?" I asked.

"My mother died when I was very young." She replied.

I was beaten by her response. I felt bad about asking, but I didn't know. Besides, I can relate to her. "Oh, I'm sorry to hear that..."

"It's okay, I barely remember her," Ai says. "My father told me that she was an intelligent woman, kind, and caring; she had great wisdom from what he said."

"Mhm, sounds like a woman with experience."

She laughed at my comment; thankfully, she noticed my sense of humor a little. It was weird—I hardly know her—but I already feel like I can be myself around her. Her energy makes me feel light and calm. I feel comfortable and emotionally safe when I'm around her. I've been missing that feeling for a while.

"She must have; I wish I could've at least been around her more before she died. I never really had those moments of having a mother." Ai said.

"Even if you never had that mother and daughter experience, she will always be in your heart and spirit." I told her, giving her grace and a peace of mind.

"Thank you, I know she is," Ai says. "I want to say I'm sorry for acting the way I did when you came here."

"You don't have to apologize, Ai. You want to protect your home and your father. I understand and respect that; you can't trust anyone nowadays. It seems like nobody has honor anymore."

"Thank you for understanding, Genji. Even though Shinano is a great town, and a safe place, you never know."

"Agreed."

We stopped the conversation for a moment, still looking at the beautiful view in the backyard.

"But what about you? What's your story?" Ai asked, making a new conversation.

"My childhood is a blur; I don't remember," I say to her, "The only childhood I cherished the most was with my father in Koawa. I was very young when I came here."

"How old were you?" She asked

"I was only ten years old. When I was twelve, my father started training me in martial arts and teaching me everything there was to know about the way of the samurai, honor, and discipline. That's when I knew about the Majo Clan, and he told me that one day I would be their leader." And that day never came, well—not yet at least. I don't know; being a samurai or leader wasn't my priority. The way things happened after my father's death. I knew those terms were bad.

"You know, speaking of that, how's everything back in Koawa? After the incident." Ai asked, changing the subject once again.

" The year after my father passed, everything changed, I don't know if it was for the good or worse." I say, " I wasn't the leader since I was still to young. My father's partner and I guess my mentor after he died, Tano, was the leader. But for those two years, they were doing nothing. Nothing to plan and stop Takashi and The Rudo Clan from what they did. I called Tano out for it, and we had a big argument that made me leave Koawa for good I left Koawa to seek my mission and handle it myself. I haven't been home in five years."

"What were you doing in those six years?" She asked me.

"Training and preparing for the mission that I set for myself:

to kill the man who took everything from me, the man who is responsible for the demons I've faced these past seven years."

"Takashi Kuri is a powerful person, don't you think you should get your people from Koawa to help you?"

"Me leaving probably caused bad blood between me and the Majo Clan and Tano, I'm afraid to even show my face there."

"But that's your home and your family, I'm sure they will understand."

"I don't know, if I'm being honest, I regret leaving. I let my emotions get the best of me, which made me lose to Takashi."

"I'm no samurai expert, but I'm sure you know you can learn from your mistakes, accept that you're not perfect, improve your weaknesses, and turn them into strengths," Ai said to me, " As I look at you and feel your energy, I know you have a good heart. You're well-minded, well-spoken, and have a lot of wisdom for a man your age."

"Thank you, Ai. My wisdom comes from my father. I'm twenty-four years old, and I see I still have a lot of learning to do, a lot of healing, and a lot of improving. I feel like I can finally move on after I complete this mission."

"I have news for you, Genji; you just completed the number one step into self-improvement. You admitted you're not perfect."

"There you too are!" says Shiro as he returns home. Both of us get up from the bench, surprised at Shiro's presence.

"Hello, Father." Said Ai

"Good afternoon, Mr. Hamasaki," I added.

"Oh, please, Genji. You can call me Shiro."

"How was work, Father?" asks Ai.

"Same old, same old. But I wanted to ask you, Ai, if you could go to the supermarket and get eggs? I'm making tempura tonight."

"Okay, I will."

"Oh, bring Genji with you; I'm sure he'll love to explore more."

"Only if he wants to, Father, I don't want to force him..."

"Oh no, it's no trouble, I would love to come," I said

I could tell it excited Ai, with a slight smile on her face. She began to walk inside to leave the house, and I followed her, walking past Shiro.

"Okay, you two have fun now!" says Shiro.

—

We are now walking in the town of Shinano; the streets are busy and alive. People walking around the sidewalks, and on the roads. I was inlighted by the fresh smell of Shinano—smelt better than most places. This was one of the towns where civilians walked with less commotion, as everyone walked with their ordinary days, as local cars drove around. I heard a lot about Shinano, but I have never been here until now. This town was very peaceful, as everything was normal and there was no heartache. I suddenly began to notice looking at me, from infront, and across of me. It wasn't anything bad, but I saw people talking with one another while staring.

"You're quite famous here. Everyone knows who you are." Said Ai, noticing what I noticed.

"I can see that." I replied to her. It does make sense. I was the son of one of the most know Samurai warriors in Japan. I wasn't surprised by this.

"Does that bother you?" Ai asked. "You know, being known because of your father's impact on everyone here and because you're a samurai and a Sato. And now that he's gone, you have a lot of pressure, and people look at you differently."

"I always felt pressure When my father told me about the history of his clan and Koawa, from that day forward, I realized I had the responsibility to honor his legacy."

"Is that why this mission that you're seeking is so important? For your father's legacy." She asked.

"Yes, his legacy greatly impacted my life like it did others, so it's my job to protect it. You wouldn't understand..."

Ai looked at me, defensive. "I do understand, Genji."

"Really? How so?"

"Just because I'm a woman and not a samurai doesn't mean I don't have the pressure to follow a loved one's honor. When my mom died, my father was always hard on me growing up. I felt like I always had the pressure to live up to my mother's legacy because of how much she impacted my father's life. I'm twenty-three years old, and I feel like I haven't achieved that yet. Not saying that my father doesn't value me as his daughter, I want to make him proud. Like you want to make your father proud by completing this mission you seek so dearly, I want to make my father proud by living up to my mother's legacy. So, even though our motive is different, it's pretty much the same, Genji."

I should've had said that. I feel awful now. "I didn't mean to offend you, I'm sorry " I said..

"You didn't...hey look, we're here."

We arrived at the supermarket. The name was Kio Blossom Market. I had never been to a supermarket before since Koawa was far from the local places. We planted our food. But first time for everything.

—

Later that night,we were all sitting down at home to eating dinner. It was nice, and amazing. The tempura was out of this world. Ai and I cooked it together. This was indeed my first time cooking, but it was a pleasant experience, especially with her.

Shiro laughed hysterically while we were at the table eating as he was telling an interesting story about Ai's childhood. "So, when Ai was thirteen, she was in a little group performing at her school. They were singing, dancing, and everything was going well."

"Father, please don't continue," says Ai as she begs him not to continue the story.

"No, no, this is the best part!" He says, ignoring her request. " Her part comes, and she's in front of the entire audience, and she froze up, not saying a word. And out of nowhere, SHE PISSES HER PANTS ON STAGE!!!" says Shiro as he hysterically laughs. I smiled slightly, chuckling as I looked between Shiro and Ai; She is looking down in embarrassment, as Shiro continues to laugh.

"Father, that's not funny...that was embarrassing," Ai said, angrily.

"Oh, come on honey, it was eighteen years ago. It's better to laugh at it than to cry."

"It could've been worse; you could've done something way worse than urinate on yourself," I added.

"EXACTLY! She could've SHAT ON YOURSELF INSTEAD!!" Shiro laughs hysterically once again.

Ai, being done with the conversation "You're so annoying!"

"I love you too, honey...how do you like the food, Genji?" Shiro asked me, changing the conversation.

"Oh, it's amazing, Shiro." I replied to him.

"I'm glad you like it," Shiro says, "Ai is one hell of a cook, isn't she?""Father, stop...I try."

"Why stop? Genji needs to know what is he getting himself into when he marries you." "Father!" Ai blushes. I'm flattered by the comment, even though Shiro didn't say it me, I kinda blushed aswell.

"Oh, come on. We're all adults here," Shiro says. " You see, Genji, when I met her mother, it was love at first sight. I knew she was the one the moment I saw her."

"Father, I don't think Genji is focused on relationships right now," Ai adds. " The man has too much going on in his life."

"I never really thought that whole thing just yet, but maybe I'll consider it. At the right time, with the right person," I stare at her intensely, letting her know, maybe—it could be her. She looked at me, smiling as her cheeks turned bright red.

"So Genji, I was thinking tomorrow, maybe you would want to come with me to my job... I'm sure you'll like it very much," says Shiro.

These are so kind, nice, and loving. I will never forget what they have done for me. Saving my life. But, even though I felt free, mentally and physically, there was that one thing still on my mind.

"I have to leave, Shiro..." I told him. This caused silence around the table, leaving Shiro and Ai in surprise by my random burst out.

"What do you mean?" asks Shiro.

"Tonight is my last night here; tomorrow morning, I will be on my way and head back to Raintoku to complete my mission," I told them the news.

"What? You can't leave!" says Shiro.

"I'm sorry, Shiro, but this mission is important to me, for my people, and for my father."

"It's only been a day; you're still not completely healed, Genji. Please rethink this. You're going to get hurt again." Shiro tried his hardest to insist me on staying, but my decision was already finalized. It hurt to leave here, but I had a job to do.

"Not this time. I know what to expect now, and Takashi will not expect me again." I say, " I'm sorry to both of you, but I must finish this."

Suddenly, Ai slams her napkin onto her plate, gets up, and rushes to her room, slamming the door. Shiro and I looked at each other in concern. What I said made her upset. Damn...I'm sorry Ai, I really am. Shiro quickly gets up and walks toward Ai's room to check on her. I stand up from the table, now feeling sorry about all of this. But, no time for sorrow, I need to get ready and get my things. I then entered the room I was staying in, grabbing all of my old, rusty gear including my katana. I head back into the living room as Shiro comes out of Ai's room. He walked to me, telling the updates of what happened.

"Give her some time...it's been a while since she had friends to talk to," says Shiro. "I understand, I didn't mean to upset her." I told him.

"Oh no, it's okay; you have a job to do; we understand that."

"Shiro, thank you for everything: saving my life, welcoming me into your home, and making me feel human." I said to Shiro.

"You are very welcome, Genji. After you've finished everything, you are always welcome to come back and live with us. Ai
would be so happy."

"Thank you, I most definitely will, sir."

We both go in for a warm hug, embracing each other's new
bond. I wished I could do the same with Ai, but I understand
that she's upset. I don't know how long I will be gone, and now
that I'm better mentally. I accept death. If I lose again, then I
will accept it and go up into the heavens where my father is staying. But I know that won't happen because I know this outcome
will be different. I just want to, in case, tell Ai my intentions
with us both, in a romantic way.

Me and Shiro let go of our hug, and Shiro said something
that really opened up a new piece of mind. "You know, God bless
your father. If he'd seen the man you've become, he would be so
proud."

"I hope so." I said to him, thinking back when my father told
me that was already proud of me, before he died.

Something quickly interrupts the conversation. A strange
object is thrown from the window. "What was that?" says Shiro
confused. I was confused by this too.

I begin to walk forward to the object and took one good look
at it. My eyes widened, my heart sunk down to my stomach, and
all of the tension rises as I found out that the object was a
grenade.

"RUN!" I yell. I try to run and grab Shiro out of the way, but
I fail as the grenade goes off.

Screaming occurs in the background. After a few minutes
of unconsciousness, I slowly woke up, but everything was still
blurry. Everything started to quickly sink in. Everything is
slowly unblurred as I looked around. Walls are torn apart,
windows broken, and fire is everywhere, burning what's left in
the house. I overhear everyone in Shinano screaming and
fighting. We were under attack. I looked to my right and see
Shiro on the ground. I quickly get up, in pain from the explo-

sion—but I managed. I turned him around; Shiro is unresponsive.

"Shiro! SHIRO WAKE UP!" I screamed. Shiro doesn't respond. I quickly checks Shiro's pulse and doesn't feel anything. Dear god, it can't be. No, no, no, it can't fucking be; Shiro was dead.

Three samurai come into the house, seeing me and Shiro's body.

"We found the Black Samurai;" Said one of the samurai. " We're now taking him into Sir Takashi,"

Fucking Takashi, he's the cause of all of this. You piece of shit! I then screamed in rage and rushed toward the samurai. All three begin to attack, but even with my injuries, I overpowered these motherfuckers. I took one of their katanas and slices the samurai's neck, blood rushing out of their system as they fall to the ground. One of them goes for my body, trying to tackle me and made me drop my katana. I took them by their back, picked them up with all of my strength, and dropped them on my left knee as I raised them up, breaking their back. The last member gets a lucky shot and slices me in the back. I punched them and grabbed them by their neck, picking them up off their toes. Without hesitation, snaps their neck with my bare hands, like a fucking twig.

Their body falls to the ground. I breathe heavily, in full rage as my eyes saw red. I suddenly think about Ai, I quickly rushed to her room, breaking down the door, and saw her on the ground. No, no,no please be alive, oh god, please be alive. I went for her body, checking her pulse. She is still breathing and has a pulse, oh thank you god. I picked her up and exits the room. As I go, I stopped to see the town. Destruction, bodies everywhere, buildings destroyed, and members from the Rudo Clan are killing innocents. Takashi, you crossed the fucking line. This beautiful town, with lovely people—now destroyed in ashes.

I run out of the house, going through a open way towards the back. I run to the forest as far as I could without getting recognized. I don't look back; I kept running without stopping as I am holding Ai in my arms. My breaths are heavy, and tears continue to run down my face. The tears turn into anger; this isn't my first time feeling this type of emotion. Takashi has started a war, and now my grief has turned into vengeance once again. There was only one place I knew that would help Ai. I didn't wanted to come to this, but I had no choice.

Koawa, I'm coming home.

CHAPTER 5

THE AMBUSH CHRONICLES

I ran quickly through the forest, with Ai still lying in my arms. I decided to stop in my tracks. I gasp for air like a fish newly taken from the water. I looked down at Ai, seeing she's still breathing but is badly hurt. Genji I took the time to look around to see I we were being followed by any Rudo Clan members. With no one else in sight, I begin to walk the rest of the way.

—

After hours of walking, I finally reached my destination. Just one more mile away, I saw my home, Koawa. Out of nowhere I got a feeling shame and remorse by looking at the village from afar. This was a bad idea: I thought, but seeing Ai like this, I had no choice. So, I shakes it off and continued walking.

When I reached the village, every single person noticed me carrying Ai, and badly hurt. Civilians are shocked and confused and started to point fingers. I don't pay any attention to everyone and kept walking straight.

"Genji?" someone speaks. I hear it and looked around for the person who called my name. As I looked, I saw an old friend, "Tano," I say.

Tano quickly walked toward me, seeing me with Ai. Looking

at him closely, he hasn't changed much physically. The only thing was that he finally had facial hair, and his hair was much longer.

"Jesus fucking Christ, what happened?" Said Tano

"Listen, no time to explain. Forget me; this woman is badly hurt and needs help." I told him

"Yeah, hold on...Hey, call the medics now!" yells Tano.

The medics from the village come to get Ai, they took her away from my arms.

"They're taking her to the emergency home," Said Tano "By the looks of it, you need treatment too."

"I'm fine." I said

"You don't look fine; you look like you've been through hell." "I told you I'm fine, Tano. I'm just worried about her."

"Well, it's going to be a minute for them to see if everything is okay with her. You need to go over and get checked, or at least get some rest while you're at it."

"I already said that I was fine, Tano, I don't need no rest," I said, but angrily

Tano laughs. "Nothing has changed, you're still stubborn."

"Excuse me?" I asked defensively.

"You must have a lot of nerve to come back here after abandoning your people, your home, and your group for five whole years."

"You know why I left, Tano."

"Aw, don't use that excuse, Genji, you weren't the only one that went through a loss, we all did. We lost hundreds of our men, and innocent people that day."

"At least I was the only one trying to do something about it," I said.

Tano stays quiet, looking at me as he put the pieces together from what I've been doing for those five years. "You went to Raintoku, didn't you? To find Takashi? How can you be so reckless?" He said to me " Doing something like that was dangerous, especially by yourself. Takashi is not someone to just go and kill just like that. This man has years of training. You were not ready."

"I'm not here for a pep talk, Tano." I interrupted him. "And don't give me any samurai lecture like you cared about me. Fourteen years ago, when I first got here, you were against me. Calling me an outsider, an outcast, saying I don't belong here, right? Well, this outsider tried to avenge and honor your beloved friend's legacy, which so happens to be my father."

"That was fourteen years ago, Genji, I don't think of you like that anymore, and you know it. If I did, I would've kicked your ass out of this village when I first saw you with that woman. You're family, and you will always be."

I brush off all of the grudges that happened many years ago. It wasn't the time to argue. I can't take my anger out on Tano or myself.

"I need to know what happened. Tell me everything," says Tano.

I closed my eyes, breathing as much to release all of the stress within me and reveal the truth. "I went to Raintoku, killed most of Takashi's men, and tried to stop him, but he stopped me. Then that woman's father saved my life and took me back to their home in Shnano. Takashi and the Rudo Clan found out I was alive and ambushed the entire town and killed hundreds, including her father."

"Does she know?" asks Tano.

"No, she was unconscious the whole time it happened. I don't know what to do now, Tano, she lost her father because of me...hose people died because of me. I had the chance to stop Takashi and I failed."

"You can't blame yourself, Genji," Tano adds.

"Then who can I blame, Tano? None of this would've happened if it wasn't for me."

"You know Genji, what I noticed from you. Even though your father taught you, the only person that was hard on you was you."

"If you're not hard on yourself, you will never get better."

"Wrong, Genji. If you are hard on yourself, you will stop yourself from getting better," says Tano.

His words hit me like a double-edged katana—those exact words from what my father said to me. It all comes full circle, and I never took that advice seriously. I should've; maybe I wouldn't have lost to Takashi. But, like Ai said, I'm not perfect, and I know that.

———

"Harold, I see that you found the dojo." Said Ken

Harold turns around as he is in the Majo dojo, looking around at the pictures and The Majo Clan logo on the wall. "Oh, Mr. Sato, I'm sorry. I didn't mean to come in here; I was just looking at the place," says Harold.

"It's okay, Harold, I was going to show you the dojo sooner, but here we are," says Ken Sato.

Ken walked up to Harold, meeting up on the mat in the center. "So, this is where you guys train to fight bad guys?" Harold asked.

"Well yes, but not necessarily bad guys. As samurai of this village, we protect it and stop possible threats that could cause any harm to our people. And for us to stay in shape and well-trained, we train here."

"Oh cool, it would be awesome to be a samurai."

"It takes years of training and discipline."

"How old were you when you became a samurai?" asks Harold.

"At fourteen years old. My father was a samurai but passed away when I was very young. So, he didn't get the chance to train me. But then I met my sensei, Hajime. He took me in and trained me."

"Didn't you say that you trained with someone?"

"Yes, his name was Takashi Kuri. We grew up together, we were like brothers, and we trained together."

"Then you guys fought and then stopped being friends?"

"It's more complicated than that," says Ken.

"How complicated?"

"Let's just say we viewed things differently as we got older and went our separate ways."

"Is he still alive?"

"I don't know."

"He is a samurai still?"

"Probably."

"Oh! Is he a bad guy now?"

"Okay, look! Enough with all the questions."

"Sorry..."

"It's okay. I was looking for you earlier because I wanted to talk to you about something."

"What is it?"

Ken walks toward Harold slowly. "You have been here for a month now and I just want to know if you enjoy being here," says Ken.

"Yeah, I love it here. It's cool, everyone is nice, and I get to learn tons of new things."

"That's good...I don't want you to be somewhere you don't enjoy, especially with everything that happened to you."

"Yeah, I do miss my mom and dad a lot...I do wish they were here," says Harold.

"I know you do. And I hope I'm doing a good job guiding you in the right direction and helping you with anything you need."

"Oh yeah, you're not doing so bad. You're cool; you're like a superhero, fighting crime, and stopping bad guys."

"Thank you," says Ken.

"Do you have kids? I bet they're lucky to have you as a dad!" asks Harold.

The smile on Ken's face fades away as Harold asks the

question. "I was going to have kids, but God had different plans for me, I guess."

"What happened?" asks Harold.

"Three years ago, I met this woman. She was so amazing, beautiful, and kind. We loved each other so much that we got married, and she was pregnant. I was excited to be a father; I wanted my kid to have what I didn't when I was growing up."

"So, what happened?"

"I'm not going to go into full detail, but to keep it short, my wife died giving birth to our child, and the child died as well."

"Oh, I'm sorry..."

"No, it's okay. It still hurts, but I learned to accept it and move on with my life."

"Well, you would've been a great dad, Mr. Sato; that kid would've been so lucky to have you. If you were my dad, I would be the luckiest kid in the world!" says Harold.

"I'm glad you said that; how do you feel about me adopting you?"

A surprised expression crosses Harold's face. "You want to adopt me? Like I would be your son?" Harold asked in shock.

"Yeah, but it's totally up to you and I don't want you to feel pressured into doing something you don't want to do."

Harold runs and hugs Ken. Ken is surprised but hugs him back. "So, I'll take that as a yes," says Ken.

As they pull away from each other, tears begin to run down Harold's face in happiness. "Thank you, Mr. Sato!"

"You don't have to call me that anymore, call me father..."

"Thank you, father."

After minutes of hugging, they both parted ways from

the hug. "Does this mean I can be a samurai?" asks Harold.

"Yes and no, you're too young, but I would be happy to train you and teach you the importance of martial arts and being a samurai. That way you will be ready when the time comes."

"Awesome!"

"But now, we need to change your name."

"Why? I like my name," says, Harold.

"I know, but for you to fit in more, you would need a name that fits into our ways ."

"Well, okay. Can I pick out my name? I can be called something like Leo, Axel, Genji, or Ace..." A light began to hit Ken as one of the names attracted his interest.

"What about the name Genji?" Asked Ken.

"Genji? That name sounds cool! Can we do that one?" Harold asked

"Of course! I like that name as well. Genji Sato has a ring to it."

CHAPTER 6

BLOODLINES OF HONOR

I n Raintoku, the remaining members travel back to home base, entering the building. As they walk inside, they encounter Takashi, who stands by the entrance.

"That was quick, I didn't expect you all to come back so soon, but I see you don't have Genji Sato," says Takashi.

"No, we don't," says one of the members. "So, what happened? And don't bullshit me."

"We went there and took out the entire town but, he got away."

Takashi stands with a blank face and doesn't respond. One of the members kneels directly on the ground, bowing to Takashi.

"We apologize, sir..."

Takashi takes a few steps forward to the member, and gently puts his hands on the member's shoulder.

"Stand," says Takashi. The member proceeds to get up, not casually, but in fear. As he gets up and is now face-to-face with Takashi, Takashi suddenly grabs the member by the throat and lifts him off the ground.

The member gasps for air, struggling to breathe. Takashi, without hesitation, snaps his neck and throws him onto the ground. The others are in shock but don't say anything.

"YOU ALL ARE WORTHLESS!" yells Takashi as he screams in rage at his samurai. "WHAT DO YOU TAKE ME FOR? A FOOL! YOU ALL HAD ONE JOB AND YOU COULDN'T EVEN DO THAT! DO YOU KNOW HOW MANY SAMRUAI I'VE KILLED? HOW MANY VILLAGES I'VE AMBUSHED? I'VE TRAINED YOU ALL TO BE THE BEST! AND YOU'RE TELLING ME, THAT YOU CAN'T FIND AND KILL A WANNABE SAMURAI?" Takashi takes a deep breath, the remaining member still standing, but with no words to say. "Everyone, to the conference room, NOW!" Without hesitation, everyone goes. "And somebody gets this body out of my building," says Takashi.

—

the conference room, everyone is in line as Takashi stands in front of them. "I am deeply disappointed, ashamed, and embarrassed. We have put down many samurai before, with ease. I just don't understand the struggle of taking down a man who doesn't even deserve to be called a samurai. This man is an outsider, an outcast, and most importantly, a disgrace to our culture." Everyone stays quiet.

"I can't sleep, knowing that Genji Sato is still out there breathing. But tonight, that's going to change. I know one place that he will go to."

"What place sir?" asks one of the members.

"Koawa... I will finish what I started seven years ago when I took down the entire village the first time, and we will finally put an end to the Majo Clan, and the Black Samurai. Everyone, get yourself situated because we're putting an end to this."

As the remaining members leave out of the conference room, Takashi remains standing there until he walks into his dojo, and opens a closet door, revealing what appears to be special samurai armor. Takashi takes out the armor and blows the dust off the chest-piece. He looks at the blood stains that are still a part of the armor and smiles menacingly.

—

Tano and I were running to the emergency room to check on Ai. Tano explained that the nurses checked up with Tano, telling him she was awake.

After a few moments of running, we finally arrived at the room's front door.

"She woke up a few moments ago," says Tano. "She's still a little foggy, so take it easy on her."

I nodded. Tano and I walked into Ai's room and saw the other nurses comforting her.

"Ai, you have a visitor," Tano says.

I locked eyes with her. Ai's eyes began to widen, and I quickly walked up and kneeled before her. "I'm very glad you are okay," I said.

Ai quickly hugs me tightly. Me with grace, I hug her back. "Did you bring us here?" asks Ai.

"Yes," I replied.

"What happened?" She asked.

"Shnano was under attack by the Rudo Clan. I tried my best to hold them down. I grabbed you and got us both out of there and came here."

"You guys went back there to stop them, right?"

"No, we didn't. Your safety was more important." I told her, I could do only so much. If I stayed and tried to fight off every Rudo Clan member, then It would've been the end of me.

"What about the others? They were innocent people; you couldn't just leave them."

"I had no choice, Ai. If I stayed, it would've put you more at risk. I couldn't take that chance."

"You got my father out of there, right? Where is he?" Ai asked

My face goes blank after her question. I didn't know what to say to her, as everyone in the room was silent.

"Genji? Where is my father?" Ai asks desperately. I looked up at Ai with guilt, grabbing her hand gently.

"He didn't make it, did he?" Ai added with another question. With the look on my face, and by reading the room, Ai knew the answer.

"I'm so sorry Ai, the bomb destroyed everything. I couldn't react in time to save him," I said to her, trying to get her to understand that this wasn't my fault.

The pain and sorrow began to fade out with tears for Ai. She let go of my hands and turned to the opposite side, rolled up to a ball, and began to cry. Guilt was all over inside me, eating me alive as I saw Ai broken into pieces. I got up from my knees and proceeded to leave the room.

I walked outside the front door and stood in the middle of the entrance.

"It's not your fault," Tano says as he walks up and stands next to me.

"Her father saved my life when I didn't deserve it and brought me into his home when he didn't need to," I say, "He looked after me as if I was his son...and now his life has been taken from him because of me. His blood is now on my hands, and Shnano is destroyed. I feel like everywhere I go, people's lives are at stake."

"Don't make it out to where your luck is negative. Things are sometimes out of your control; it could've happened any other way," says Tano.

"I had the chance to kill Takashi, but I failed. None of this would've happened if I just didn't let my emotions beat me. I thought I found my spirit, but I didn't. My spirit is broken. I'm broken. I owe this to my father, and I can't even do that."

"You may feel like that right now, but you will keep going. I am here to tell you that every man here, every samurai, has felt that at some point in their life. Especially your father," says Tano, "When I look at you now, I see a man whose spirit is broken trying to protect someone else's. Only one man can pick up the broken pieces, and that man is you. You don't owe it to your father; there are times in life when you have to owe it to yourself."

—

Meanwhile, Takashi and the remaining members ride their horses, on the quest to arrive at Koawa. Just a few miles away, Takashi is in the front, leading them there. Everyone is quiet; one member walks up to Takashi.

"Sir, what is exactly the plan here?" asks the member.

"Simple, when we're close, we wait until the time is right. When that comes, we take them all out," says Takashi.

"Do you think that you're going into this blind? That man that you seek to kill murdered half of our men. We are going to be outnumbered."

"Don't tell me that you're afraid."

"I just want us to think more clearly on this. If I was the leader..." Takashi stops his horse aggressively, forcing everyone else to stop as well.

"Well, you're not! You're afraid. Being afraid is for the weak, not for the men who have the strength to be better. I don't care how many there are or how many advantages they have; that's not going to stop me from completing my goal, nor should it stop you. We're close to the destination, so don't have second thoughts now. Koawa, Genji Sato, and what's left of the Majo Clan ends today, by our hands, as it should be."

Takashi then begins to move again, leaving the

members speechless. The other members begin to follow Takashi. In the distance, a stranger lurks in the bushes watching them. They hear everything that Takashi is speaking about and leave the environment, running out into the distance.

CHAPTER 7

THE VEIL OF JUSTICE

T he sun was coming up, and seeing the yellow and red in the back never got old for me. But after a few hours of reflecting and thinking, I returned to the emergency center. I walked into the room that Ai was in, opened the door, and saw her sitting up straight in the bed.

"How are you holding up?" I asked her. She slightly turned her head to face me but knew it was me, probably by my voice.

"I'm better, how about you?" asks Ai.

"I'm still alive, so that counts as something."

We both chuckled. I began to walk toward her, needing to face her closely after everything that happened. I kneel, making eye contact.

"I never thought my life would go like this. I always tried to forget about my childhood before I met my father and focus on the good times. When I told you that I didn't remember my childhood, I lied. I remember all of it."

"Genji, it's okay, I understand," Ai says.

"No, it's not okay, you almost died, and I made you lose someone that you loved, you deserve the truth. When I was ten, my real parents died. I was alone until Ken Sato came and saved my life. He took me in and adopted me. Ever since then, I always looked up to him, as my mentor, my leader, and of course as my father. When Takashi and his men came here and destroyed everything, and killed my father, I felt like I was reliving the time when I lost my other parents. I was rageful, I was bitter, and I realized no one was doing anything about it. So, I left and never came back. My main focus was to kill this man who took everything from me, and to honor my father's legacy, but I failed. I failed him, Shiro, Koawa, and you..."

Tears begin to flow down my face. Ai gently grabbed me by my hand with her right hand and gently grabbed my face with her left.

"Genji, you didn't fail me, nor my father. That man admired you and thought that you were a special human being. You didn't fail anybody. I know deep down that your father is looking down at you right now, and he is nothing but proud of you for the man you've become.. You beat yourself up over this goal, about honoring Ken's legacy, but I'm here to tell you that your father will always be remembered for the good he has done. But right now, Genji, you need to build your legacy and find your purpose in this world."

"What do you think my purpose is?" I asked her.

"You need to find out on your own. But no matter how long that takes, you will eventually find out what that is."

"How will I know?" "You'll know, I promise."

A nurse suddenly barges into the room with me and Ai. Coming in with full worrying, but kept it calm and professional, "Mr. Sato, Tano wants to see you outside; he said it is urgent!"

I was alerted. I got up and started to head out. I turned to Ai, told her I would be right back, and dashed out.

——

I came outside and noticed a stranger, Tano, and two other Majo Clan members standing in the middle of the village. "What's going on?" I asked yelling in concern.

"We're about to be under attack, Takashi knows you're here. He and his men are coming now!" says Tano.

Oh fuck, just as I needed. That man does not give up, don't he? "How can you be so sure?" I asked.

"I saw them; Takashi was screaming and yelling at his men. They were all riding their horses to come over here!" says the civilian.

"Did you hear anything he said?" I asked him.

"Yes... he said that you, Koawa, and the Majo Clan will end by their hands. As it should be." "What are we going to do, Tano? We don't know how many there are," says one of the members.

"Not too many, I know because I killed half of them when I was at Raintoku," Genji adds.

"So, they may be outnumbered." Said one of the members again.

"Indeed. Here's what we're going to do. We don't know how long until he comes, but we have a little bit of a head start. Hiro, alert all of the civilians in the village to start evacuating immediately," says Tano.

"Where are they going to go?" asks Hiro.

"A friend named Hayato in Takayama can help shelter everyone until everything is over. You alert them and call the associates to come down and bring them there. Tell him that I sent you."

"Got it, sir!" Hiro leaves quickly, preparing to alert the people in Koawa.

"Koji, alert the other members and tell them to meet us at the conference room. We need to discuss a plan on what we're going to do."

"On it, sir!" says Koji as he also leaves, as quickly as possible without hesitation and no question.

"Genji, come with me to the conference room," Tano demands. As he starts to leave, my concern rises when I think about Ai.

"Wait, what about Ai?" I asked.

"Everyone will be transported to Takayama, and they will take all the medical patients to their hospitals. She will be fine, I promise. We have no time to waste. Let's go."

—

Hiro gets on the intercom. Everything is happening at a fast paste, but Hiro stays calm.

"Attention everyone in Koawa, this is not a drill. The Majo Clan is transporting everyone to Takayama until further notice. Please only bring belongings that you can carry meet in the middle of the village"

Everyone begins to bring their things, leaving their homes, confused and wondering what's going on. As they all meet outside, Hiro arrives.

"Everyone, may I have your attention? As you heard, you will be sent to Takayama until further notice."

"What's happening? is the village under attack?" asks one of the civilians.

"I can't explain what's going on right now, but I assure you all that everything is under control. The people that will take you all will be here any second."

Within seconds, Hiro hears vehicles driving into the village. "Here they are..." Hundreds of Kei park side by side, ready for everyone to get on. "Okay everyone, get on each truck, if you don't fit in one find another," says Hiro. People begin to get on the trucks calmly.

Everyone from the medical center leave the building, and nurses help the patients get on the trucks. Ai walks and looks around to find Genji, the nurses advise her to come with them to the trucks.

Ai sees Hiro and walks toward him in a worried manner. "What's going on? Where's Genji?" asks Ai.

"He's with Tano, he's going to be okay."

"Takashi is coming, isn't he?"

Hiro stares at her blankly. "You have to get on the

truck now," he says. A nurse gently grabs Ai and pulls her to one of the trucks.

"Make sure you all kill him, and don't let anything happen to Genji," says Ai as she gets on the truck. When everyone has boarded the trucks, they leave Koawa, proceeding to Takayama. Hiro watches them leave, making sure they leave in safety. It isn't until he trucks are far away and barely noticeable to them that Hiro walks away and starts heading to the conference room.

—

All the members of the Majo Clan were standing, talking, and waiting for everything to be discussed in the conference room. Me and I were on the side of the room when Hiro arrived.

"Tano, everyone left; the village is now clear," says Hiro. Alright, perfect. Excellent job, Hiro."

"Thank you, sir." Hiro walked away, joining the rest of the members in the center.

"We are now in a personal crisis. At any moment, Takashi will come and bring Koawa to hell," Tano says, "We must think of a plan quickly!"

"I have an idea, but if we're going to do this, I must lead this fight," I told Tano. He then chuckled at my suggestion.

"You know I can't allow that."

"What's the reason behind that?" I asked.

"For all these years after Ken died, I was the one who had to lead and take care of this village and organization. It took us so long to rebuild this village after what Takashi did, and they trust me, depend on me, and expect me to tell them the plan."

"This fight is not just yours; it's also mine. As you said, I owe it to myself. But to do that, I must lead this fight, Tano."

Tano thinks for a moment, slightly hesitant about my request, but later, agrees. "Okay, you'll lead, but don't make me regret this," says Tano.

"Thank you," I told him.

We both walked in front of the members, standing next to each other. "Attention!" yells Tano. The other members go quiet and turn to face us while we are on a slightly tall stage.

"As you all may know, the Rudo Clan plans to attack us again. But fortunately, we know they're coming," says Tano.

"So, what's the plan, sir?" asks one of the members.

"As of right now, and during battle, I'm going to make Genji Sato take the lead on this one." After the comment, the members whisper to each other in confusion.

"I know this seems odd, but as you all may not know, Genji Sato is the son of Ken Sato. He's faced Takashi before, so he has more experience than all of us. I am confident that he will lead us to victory, and you all should be too. Go ahead, Genji."

I walked in front of Tano, staring at all of the members as they stared at me back. This was my moment, my time. After all of those years of becoming a ronin, a rebel. Having such anger in my heart, I can finally become what my father prepared me to be —a leader.

"Majo Clan, we are here today to make a statement, to show that we are not going to back down from this fight. Before I came here, I was lost, scared, and alone. Ken Sato saved my life, brought me here, and raised me to be the man I am now. When I look at you all, I see bravery, will, and potential to be the best version of yourselves, better than you were yesterday or the day before. We are here to fight for Koawa and the people who are in need. We plan to stand right behind the village, waiting for them to arrive. When they do come, we will be right there waiting for them. The world will remember this day, and the world will remember us. Now, let's go make history!"

Everyone shouts with excitement, all gearing up and preparing for battle. Tano walks up to me, impressed. "Not bad, kid."

"Thank you. Now let's go," I say, insisting on leaving the conference room.

"Wait, wait, wait, don't tell me you're going without any armor."

"My armor was destroyed at Raintoku," I said.

"Don't worry, we have a spare over here."

Tano walked over to a big door on the right of the stage. He opened the door, revealing three different samurai armor. "Choose whatever you like," Tano insists. "Also, Genji, I have something else for you."

I turned to see, and what I saw shocked me. "Is that..." I said.

"Yes, Genji, this is the katana that belonged to Ken."

I thought it was impossible. I thought the katana was lost. It looked brand new, with my father's blue tap strap all over the holder. "You still have this?" I asked.

"I kept it hidden, and nobody touched it after he passed. But now I want to give it to you." I took the katana, gently holding it. I stared at the Katana and the Majo Clan emblem on the blade.

"Why are you giving this to me?" I asked.

"When Ken's wife was pregnant, he told me that when his child gets older, he wanted them to have this, as his sensei had welded this. Now, his dream has come true; he's looking down right now, seeing his child welding his katana."

"Thank you, Tano...Any more surprises I should look out for?" I asked.

"Not at the moment, but the time will come. Start getting ready; I'll be right outside the room.

—

I walked out of the conference room wearing my brand-new samurai armor. The black metal pieces were shiny and modern, and my helmet fitted me perfectly.

"You look good," says Tano, looking up and down at me. "It's probably good enough to beat Takashi," Tano adds.

"This armor is just protection; my skills and mindset will do the talking."

"That's what I like to hear. Are you ready? This is the moment we have been waiting for." "I am; I won't make the same mistake as last time. After this, he and Rudo Clan will be no more. This is seven years in the making, Tano. He started this, and we're going to finish it."

CHAPTER 8

THE VEIL OF VENGEANCE

Me and the rest of the Majo Clan dressed up in our armor, stand behind the village waiting.

"Genji...Are you okay? You're zoning out," says Tano.

"I'm fine, I'm just thinking..." I replied.

"About what?"

"About how is this going to end? I'm already imagining it."

"How do you think this will turn out?" He asked me.

"Us winning, and Takashi dead by my hands. Before, I was reckless, but now I have everything planned out."

"Don't think so hard about it, Genji. Our men are very skilled!"

"You can be the most skilled samurai in the world, but if your mindset is not there, none of that matters." I tell him.

After the conversation, one of the members notices a group of people walking up into the distance. "They're here," says one of the members.

The Rudo Clan has arrived. Takashi noticed us standing behind the village, blocking off the entrance. I proceeded to walk forward toward the Rudo Clan as the Majo Clan followed behind me. Both clans came to a stop twenty feet away from each other. I walked in front as Takashi got off his horse and walked in front also. We both faced off, in both ends wanting each other so much, and now we are able to grant each other's wish.

"You thought you could pull the same trick, but as you can see, we're now prepared," I say.

"I see, but that's not going to stop me from finishing my job," says Takashi. "Tano, you're letting this imposter of a samurai lead you? Pathetic."

"Your conflict is not with him, so focus on me," I yelled, demanding him to respect me.

"I focus on who I want; I don't have any respect for you." Said Takashi

" You never had any respect; you're nothing but a coward." I replied.

"We'll see who's the coward soon enough. RUDO CLAN DRAW!"

Takashi and the Rudo Clan draw their katanas and go into fight positions. I went ahead and told the group to draw theirs. Both Clans are now ready for battle; it's only a matter of time before one of them makes the first call to attack. Takashi and I look across at each other with death stares. Takashi, waiting impatiently, calls the first attack; he and the Rudo Clan charge. As they're charging, me and the Majo Clan begin to chargeback, and we all go to war.

The Majo and Rudo Clans battle it out, giving everything they got. Minutes felt like hours; the Majo Clan had the advantage. As I was hitting some blows off of some of the Rudo Clan members, I was also looking for the man I sought the most. After beating and killing every single Rudo Clan member that came my way, Takashi and I finally came face to face.

"I'm going to do what I should've done before. I hope they remember you," says Takashi.

"I'd like to see you try," I replied back to him.

Takashi leaps at me, throwing heavy blows with his katana, but I block and weave away dodging them easily. I been through this before, and I refuse to make the same mistake again.

—

In Takayama, the civilians arrive, the trucks are parked, and Hayato, a friend of Tano, greets them.

"Hello, everyone; please follow me to the safe house where you all will be staying," says Hayato.

The people leave the trucks and begin to follow Hayato to the safe house. Ai gets out, in distress about Genji. As she follows the rest, she then stops. She begins to think, coming up with a certain plan but is hesitant to do it. She looks around and notices the car keys still in the ignition of one of the trucks. She lets her intuition and thoughts win and walks back to the trucks. She quickly rushes into the truck that has the keys still inside and begins to drive off. Hayato and the rest see her driving away, they all yell and try to run after her, but she's already on the road.

—

As Taskashi and I clashed our katanas, Takashi pulled away, kicking me off balance and causing me to take a step back.

"Glad you're putting up a better fight this time, it will make your death more memorable," Takashi shouts. I scream, wanting to kill him properly this time. Takashi once again leaps at me, and we clashed once again.

Takashi side-kicks me off my feet, then jumps high to impale me with his katana, but I quickly dodged, separating himself from Takashi. I think for a second, grabbing something from my pockets—my Tanto. I throw it at Takashi, hitting him in his right eye as he screams in pain. I run up at him, kicking him off his feet.

Takashi is down, and I stand my ground. Takashi, furious, quickly gets up, taking the Tanto out of his eye—with blood quickly flowed down. He draws back his katana and viciously screams as he rushes toward me. Takashi goes for a swing with his sword, but I dodged it with ease, then counters his attack by hitting Takashi and breaking a piece of his armor. Takashi is down on one knee, looking at me with anger.

"Your anger clouds your judgment, Takashi, I thought you were a samurai." I say to him, taunting. The taunting angers Takashi, and he gets up and clashes with me. Takashi goes for a big blow but I see it coming before it happens and counterattacks by slicing Takashi in his left arm where the armor piece was broken off.

Takashi, bleeding from his arm, proceeds to go for another attack. Takashi catches me by cutting me in the face. I stepped back and touched. I'm not fazed by, as I went and left a big grin at him.

"Is that all you got?" I yelled.

Takashi rushes, going for another blow with his katana. I block it with my katana, pushing Takashi away, moving forward, hit Takashi in the stomach as blood gushes out rapidly. Takashi can barely stand up, but pulls through, still willing to use all his strength to keep fighting.

I stand in front of him, seeing Takashi badly hurt, but I don't feel any remorse.

Suddenly, screaming happens in the background. I look from afar, and see the Majo Clan cheering and screaming as they have won the fight between the Rudo Clan. Takashi, feeling defeated, looks down at his hands as they're full of blood.

"It's over, Takashi...You've lost. Stand down," I say, encouraging him to accept his defeat.

Takashi is unable to accept the defeat. He looked at me with anger in his eyes and heart. He screamed in rage and aggressively ran at me. He went for a last blow, but I swept-kicked Takashi off his feet. Takashi was on the ground, and I pierced Him in the back with my katana without hesitation, pulling it back out.

The sounds of pain and agony come from Takashi's voice,

unable to stand up. I cleaned the blood off of my katana, putting it away. After everything that I went through, I finally got my revenge and proceeded to walk away from Takashi.

"What are you doing, huh? Finish me off! This is what you wanted! For Ken's sake! I will be seeing him in hell!"

I stopped in my tracks, turning around to look at Takashi for one last time.

"Even though you took my father from me, the one thing that you haven't taken was my spirit...You tried to turn me into something I'm not. I realized that I have a purpose in this world: to protect people who can't protect themselves from people like you. I'm not going to finish you off. I want you to sit there and die slowly as you watch me and my group cheer in victory. And I want you to always know that Genji Sato, the Black Samurai, beat you for all eternity."

I walked away, leaving Takashi to sit and slowly bleed out.

As I approached the rest of the group, they noticed me, and they all cheered at me with open arms, running up and picking me up as I led them to victory.

A truck suddenly begins to approach us. We are confused and try to get a good look at who it might be. The truck comes to a stop, the person gets out of the truck, and it's none other than Ai. The reveal sunk my heart into my stomach; I was in disbelief. They all put me down as I ran at her. Ai breaks down in tears of happiness and proceeds to run at me as well.

We both come to the middle and hug each other. Ai cries in my arms as she is holding me tightly.

"What are you doing here?" I asked.

"I couldn't stop worrying about you, Genji. I just needed to see if you were okay," says Ai. I then gently grabbed her face, bringing her closer. "I'm fine; I'm glad you're okay," I say.

"I'm better now that I'm with you," Ai replied to me.

We both looked at each other, getting lost in each other's eyes. I have been wanting to do this ever since I laid eyes on her, leaned in to gracefully kiss her, and Ai kissed me back. Both of us embrace each other's love. We held onto each other as we still had each other on our lips and never let go.

EPILOGUE: ONE WEEK LATER

"The people of Koawa, thank you all for coming. As you already know, we finally won the battle between the Rudo Clan," Tano says. The people cheered for this comment and congratulated him on our victory.

"They destroyed us, took everything from us on that tragic day in 2017, but we took it back. Even though we defeated the enemy, more enemies would rise. As samurai, it's our job to fight and protect the ones who cannot protect themselves. Having a great leader beside them makes this group more vital and brings us closer together. I bring you all here today to announce our new protector of Koawa. Ladies and gentlemen, I bring you the new leader of the Majo Clan, Genji Sato, The Black Samurai." The whole audience begins to clap and cheer for my callout. I don't know why Tano called me that, but I like it. The Black Samurai has a ring to it.

I come up on stage with the utmost confidence. I shook Tano's hand, went up to the people, and said something I'd wanted to say for a while.

"First, I would like to thank you all for attending and accepting me as your new protector. You may not know who I am, but that's okay because I didn't know myself either. Before, my life was upside down; I was lost, scared, and didn't know what life would bring me. I know when I arrived here, some people didn't accept me, not yet, at least. I was called an outsider, an outcast, and a wannabe samurai, and I would be lying if I said those things didn't bother me because they did. But as time passed, I showed I could be a part of this. When our former leader, our protector, my father, died, I lost myself. I was rageful and bitter. I lost sight of who I was and everything my father taught me. But now I can finally say that that's not the case anymore. I have a purpose, a purpose to be something, a symbol, and someone that the youth can look up to. I want to show that anyone can be a samurai; it just takes will, strength, discipline, and hard work. The world will remember this day as the day of a new age and hope. I am here to give you my promise and protect you from upcoming threats. These threats may be stronger than us or have the power to destroy us. No matter what, even if our enemies are stronger, more powerful, or better skilled, I will not stop fighting for my people."

The audience cheered for my speech, and all the clan members congratulated me on stage. Ai came up on stage, embracing her support for him. We held on to each other. Tano walked over with the utmost happiness in the world.

"How do you feel?" He asked me.

"I don't know; things haven't sunk in yet," I responded.

"It better sink in soon because you now have the entire village on your back depending on you. You're a protector now, a leader, and Takashi will not be the only one wanting power. Others will rise, wanting to take your place and destroy the clan to embrace their own. Are you sure you're ready for that?"

"Like I said, Tano, these enemies can be stronger, but I will not stop fighting. I will never forget what my father did for Koawa, but now it's my turn to take on this responsibility. To build...my legacy."

ACKNOWLEDGMENTS

First I want to say thank you to the person who bought the book and took the time to read it. Whether you like the book or not, thank you for giving it a chance, even though it's a novella. I came into this author career scared, because I didn't think nobody would read it or like it. But, as for my filmmaking career, I realized that I can't please everyone and my stories are not for everyone so, I'm taking that mindset into my author career. The only thing I could always do is to hear constructive criticism, learn from my errors, and move forward and be better. This book is not by any means perfect, but I still enjoyed writing this and I loved every bit of it. I can't wait to continue writing more stories in the future as I get better because I'm just getting started.

The support from my family is what made this book possible, but there's one person who really influenced my career. I remember when I was little, my brother had these homemade books that he created by himself. I remember reading every single book and got me so excited In my mind I said " I wanna do this!" For years, I always wanted to become an author, to write my own books, and now that dream is becoming a reality. I just want to thank my brother for being an inspiration of mine for my own life. I don't think I would be the person I am today if it weren't for him. Bro, if you're reading this, I love you man. Thank you for being my positive influence!

ABOUT THE AUTHOR

Jalen Tellis is an African-American author who is known for his complex storytelling.